Eighte
hours
with
capricious
Violette

EIGHTEEN HOURS WITH CAPRICIOUS VIOLETTE
Copyright © S E Fitzgereld, 2009

The right of S E Fitzgereld to be identified as author of this work has been
asserted by her in accordance with the Copyright, Designs and Patents Act 1988.

A CIP catalogue record for this book is available from the British Library.

ISBN 978-0-9555171-3-6

Published in 2009 by Intrigue Books, Millefiori Publishing, Redhill, Surrey.
info@millefioripublishing.co.uk

Design by Jonathan Spearman-Oxx
Cover photography by Neil George

Printed and bound in the UK by CPI Bookmarque, Croydon.

NOTE FROM THE AUTHOR TO THE READER

The text of this novel was completed in autumn 2008, by happy coincidence a landmark anniversary of the founding of the magnificent Mont-Saint-Michel. This awe-inspiring French treasure leaves a lasting impression on both those who live close to it and those who travel to visit it. You will find glimpses of this monument in several parts of this book but naturally nothing beats seeing the real thing.

You will also find sprinklings of French, often in conversations. I hope this authentic touch will bring you pleasure and enrich the experience (rather like the addition of *crème Chantilly* to a slice of Normandy apple tart...) You may know some *français* or very little, but relax – some phrases are explained at the back of the book. *Bon appétit!*

For Susannah and Neil with love

This book is also dedicated to Diana

Eighteen hours with capricious Violette

S E FITZGERELD

intrigue

CHAPTER 1

Thinking back, it seems to me that the whole thing came about by serendipity. There just happened to be that midsummer deluge, I just happened to dive in for an espresso, and someone happened to have abandoned their newspaper on the only free table. And perusing the damp pages of that erudite daily (the rival to my usual) I hit on her advert... which, after weeks of half-hearted searching and lacklustre results, was just what I'd been looking for. Correction – more than I'd been looking for. I guess it was not so much an advert as an invitation...

Yes, there it was, seemingly waiting for me, a veritable gem among the Classifieds: *'Parlez-vous français?'* While underneath the heading was her cute French name flaunting itself in italics at me! So, that was it: I was hooked.

Of course, I have always been a sucker for an attractive name. Must have seen hundreds of them in my career, typed or handwritten on case notes, invariably preceding the female patients associated with them, and tempting me, on occasion, to sketch a picture in my mind. And sure, over the years there have been some cracking ones: Celestine, Barbara-Lucia... Estelle... Ingrid... even a Mitzi! But never once was there a Violette.

Now with that deliciously exotic name she was on to a winner from the start, a sure-fire way to attract the attention of an Englishman vaguely contemplating the idea of moving across the Channel and wanting to brush up his French – and spice up his life a little bit. And I see it now, as clear as on that rainy morning seven months ago, her brilliantly devised *petite annonce:*

> **Parlez-vous français?** Perfectionnez votre accent avec moi, *Violette*… Conversation, grammaire, examens et études littéraires sous la direction de 'la Maîtresse'. Région Londres. Contactez V. S. Lorance. Tél: 020 8947…

Well, well, what an inviting proposition: the chance to improve my French in conversation with a prettily named and, hopefully, pretty-faced private tutor. Exactly what I was hoping for – a bit of conversation, a bit of grammar and a bit of *entente amicale*… And already – crazily! – a couple of images of Violette sprang up in my imagination. Yes, with such a name she could be the delicate, feminine type, possibly petite, fair and sweet-voiced; alternatively, she could be a shady, sulky brunettish type of Violette with a husky drawl. Either way, it seemed, she would be far more interesting to learn French with than a nameless unknown quantity put forward by one of those tuition agencies.

So I took a second look, and that was when – as if Violette wasn't appealing enough! – I noticed the *other* word, casually flung in to the penultimate line. Her masterstroke: Learn French under the guidance of 'la Maîtresse'! Now, there was a word… No, more than a word – a title, no less. Didn't it ring a bell from some period film on TV years ago? Something whispered suggestively in a lavish Rococo interior or among the topiary of a maze…

Question was: how on earth did a word like that manage to slip past the eagle eyes of the Classifieds department?

Evidently their knowledge of French wasn't up to the mark. Not that I understood the precise meaning of the term, either. But one intriguing translation kept spinning in my head: Mistress! That's what it meant: mistress. Or at least, that was one meaning. At which point I finished my coffee, rejoined the sopping Putney High Street and headed home, newspaper in hand, for a little linguistic research.

Duly dampened down on my return, it struck me there was probably a perfectly innocent explanation. Yes, logic dictated that the Violette behind the advertisement (whether shrinking or sultry!) would be calling herself a mistress in the scholarly sense. Quick check of my new bilingual dictionary, that great 2000 page tome, and there it was, plain and simple: *la maîtresse d'école* – schoolmistress or teacher. But, sixty-four thousand dollar question: what kind of schoolmistress would Violette be? She could be quite mature; even a plump, grey matron, which would, obviously, be rather disappointing. On the other hand, she could be a young teacher; attractive, intelligent, vivacious, not unlike Nicole from those classic Renault adverts. Now *she* would do nicely, I remember thinking.

Unless, of course, by that extraordinary word she was meaning something very different – as in the second definition on the page. A mistress in the classic, time-honoured sense: a duplicitous *maîtresse* involved in affairs and dangerous liaisons. Yes, maybe my first instinct in the café was right; under the guise of her French lessons, she was sending a subliminal message to wealthy, married men seeking a bit of excitement and illicit adventure. Yes, la charmante Violette just might be a glamorous temptress with flirtatious, violet-blue eyes to match her name… OK, it was a possibility, albeit a remote one.

Alternatively, and more probably, it seemed she could be an entrepreneurial type of mistress; a director of some kind, as in the *maîtresse de l'académie* suggested by the dictionary. Suddenly she appeared in my mind's eye – classy as Cathérine Deneuve, rolling up outside her language school in South Kensington, conveniently close to the Institut Français and the multitude of café-restaurants. Her private establishment would be filled with aspiring professionals and ok-yah Chelsea types, who would eagerly come after work or in the lunch hour to polish up their *français* with the inspirational Violette.

Yes, there they were: three distinct possibilities floating around my head: the schoolmistress, the seductress and the entrepreneur... and I guess I was leaning, a little hopefully, towards the third option. But further forays into *le dictionnaire* led to a couple of other possibilities, one of them really quite extreme.

She could be a sadistic, power-crazed *maîtresse*; 'une femme qui exerce une domination', as it said. A dominatrix, no less, in black leather and thigh-length boots, standing by, ready to punish her clients' linguistic faux-pas. 'Non! Imbécile! C'est incorrecte.' Crrrrrack! Surreal, absurd, crazy idea! Way too far-fetched and twisted, surely...

Coming back to earth, there was, however, the final option: that the originator of the advert was, quite simply, a *maîtresse de son sujet* – a master of French language and literature. In which case, enter the gifted academic Violette Lorance, expert in every nuance, every linguistic twist and turn of her native tongue. Now, to have private coaching with such a charming luminary of the French intelligentsia – imagine the kudos of that! Although, I did just wonder: why on earth would someone of such brilliance need to advertise in the newspaper?

So there they were – five variations on the theme of a *maîtresse*. Yet, to be honest, none of them made perfect sense to me back then – or indeed now. However, one thing was crystal clear: anyone marketing herself with such an irresistible name and title had to be a woman of flair, ingenuity and breathtaking nerve. In short, the kind of woman who knows exactly how to get herself noticed.

Of course, I didn't make contact straightaway. Lord no. That would be the sort of knee-jerk reaction of a bored, fifty-plus divorcee with nothing better going on in his life. No, the advertisements section stayed on the dining room table for a good few days, receiving the odd drop of Shiraz and meriting an occasional glance over dinner or breakfast. Casual of course but sufficient to note her local phone number; Wimbledon no less. My neck of the woods! So eventually – inevitably – temptation overcame me. It was a sunny Friday morning in mid-June, as I recall, when we had our fascinating opening conversation.

'Oui, âllo… Hello?'

Youngish voice. Thirty-something by the sound of it.

'Hello. Is that Violette Lorance?'

'Yes. How can I help you?'

Nice, attractive pitch, with a seductive French accent.

'My name's Michael Westover. I've seen your advert in the paper for private tuition and I'm considering booking some sessions starting this summer.'

'I see. And you live in the London area?'

'Putney.'

'Oh yes, Putnay. And you already speak some French? Vous parlez français?'

'Oui, Madame. Je parle le français pas mal… Well, enough to get by on holiday. In fact, I can offer an ancient O level pass if that means anything these days.'

'Oh yes. Very good.'

'But you see, I'm planning to buy a place in France, so I need

11

to be able to communicate with plumbers and electricians, and fraternise with my neighbours. In a nutshell, I need to improve my pronunciation and general fluency.'

'I understand. So you are definitely wanting private lessons – not evening classes?'

'Good heavens, no. To be honest, I've got beyond evening classes. Pretending to buy tickets at the Gare du Nord with some tongue-tied partner isn't quite my scene.'

'Yes, I understand. Lots of my clients feel this way. They like the advantage of a private session, one to one.'

Won tou won... Yes, one to one with you, Violette... The soft voice tells me you would be slim and feminine and rather petite. Could be very stimulating.

'Exactly. One to one tuition is what I'm after. By the way, what's your rate?'

'Well it starts with... Let me see, yes, it is approximately forty pounds.'

'Ah, forty – per hourly session?'

'Yes. Is that conforming to your expectation?'

I remember the charming yet slightly challenging tone.

'Well, depending on your level of service...'

'Let me explain. Usually I attend the client's home and we spend one hour with conversation, listening skills, or *grammaire*, literature... Also if you want it, we can prepare for examinations – par exemple, Alliance Française, Institute of Linguists...' (Professional, I thought, she must be the language academy type of *maîtresse*.) 'Alors, vous comprenez... my objective is for my clients to achieve excellent progress and enjoy speaking French.'

'Fine. Well, let's go ahead and book a session.'

'Certainly. I just need some details. Your profession?'

'I'm in medicine. I work in a London teaching hospital.'

'Ah...' I noticed the strange silence before she carried on hastily. 'Ac-tu-al-ly, Docteur Westover, I see from my diary that I have a lot of bookings at the moment. Yes, especially after my advertisement – the response has been considerable.'

'Ah, OK. Well, it's not urgent. Although, naturally, I'm keen to get started.'

At that point there was a change in tone at the end of the line. More wary, more defensive and distinctly more French.

'Ecoutez... The problème is that I 'ave many students who come to me for the long-terme and therefore most of my time, as you understand, is consecrated to them. And I must speak frankly with you, Docteur Westover – I prefer to accept new students who are serious with the commitment to learn and study French with me. You understand?'

'Sure. OK then, let's look at a longer-term arrangement. Just for the record, I'm not averse to taking the odd exam, having spent umpteen years studying to become a consultant.'

My trump card!

'Oh. So you are consultant.' She said it the French way: con-suel-ton.

'Yes. Consultant surgeon, actually, if that makes a difference.'

'Oui! Oui, ça fait une différence...' I remember being taken by surprise by the sudden stream of French, pretty unintelligible, except for something about the need to *modifier le tarif*. 'Alors, dans ces circonstances, docteur, cela vous fera soixante livres Sterling... You understand? Sixty pounds.'

'Sixty pounds an hour?'

'That is correct.'

'Ha-ha-ha. Very good! I see you share my sense of humour, Madame.'

'I am talking perfectly seriously.'

'You can't be. Sixty quid a go! Just now, you said forty!'

'I said perhaps. Approximately forty. But let me explain: this is my standard *tarif*, yes? And at this moment I did not have the complete picture of your work, I mean to say your *capacité professionnelle*.'

'I see. So when you have the 'complete picture', you see fit to increase your fee by fifty per cent! Well, I have to say, that strikes me as extortionate.'

'You have the liberté of your opinion.'

The breathtaking nerve! All too reminiscent of the bloody-minded French hotelier who has slapped a dubious supplement on your credit card.

'So, Madame, you're not disagreeing with me that it's a pretty extortionate practice to increase your rate for professionals – doctors, lawyers, and so on?'

'But excuse me! My *tarifs* are my *affaire* but for your information, docteur, I 'ave a number of professional clients – solicitors, actuaries, finance directors – and they are content with my service and my charges.'

'Really? So they're happy to pay you sixty quid an hour? I suppose they would be with their exorbitant fees and bonuses.'

'What they pay me is confidential, natur-al-ly.'

'Ah, yes, naturally.'

Impasse…

'Well, Madame Lorance, it really has been quite extraordinary talking to you. *Une révélation*...'

'Docteur Westover, if you prefer, you will find French tutors in the Yellow Pages. They will offer you an average price – for an average service. I hope you will find one to suit your requirements.'

Was it my imagination, or did I hear a smirk in her voice?

'Thanks. Likewise, may I wish you luck in finding a suitable doctor to fleece, if I can put it like that.'

A second's silence for that parting shot to sink in. But then she rebounded, totally unfazed.

'Thank you for your *concerne*. But what I choose to do with my other clients is entirely my *affaire*. Au revoir, docteur.'

'Au revoir. Madame.'

She was extraordinary! Justifying her outrageous scale of charges as if that were perfectly logical. Sixty quid an hour – screw that, Madame! And screw you! OK, I was frustrated and, truth be told, disappointed, because my fantasy of setting eyes on her had just evaporated into thin air.

So plan B it was. Yellow Pages... Private tutors – ha! Two-a-penny. And, unlike 'la charmante' Violette, the first agency was extremely accommodating. Home visit lined up p.d.q. with the young Danielle. Promising, promising.

At least she showed up on time – ten o'clock, Monday morning. I saw her walking up the path; early twenties and unmistakably French – olive skin, long brown hair, classic navy and red striped tee shirt and jeans. I just beat her to the front door.

'Mademoiselle Danielle? Bonjour.'

'Bonjour.'

'Entrez...'

I should have known straightaway from her body language; the way she stood with a kind of dumpy awkwardness, preoccupied with her trainers, while I closed the door, and the silence as we made our way upstairs to the living room. Not to mention the charmless manner in which she sank into the sofa.

'Ah Danielle... vous désirez le café, le thé?'

'Non, merci.' A little shrug of irritation.

Ah of course – the French don't share the English passion for constant brew-ups, nor our overactive bladders. But as for me, I was desperate for my mid-morning caffeine boost. I remember catching Danielle's rather sullen, disappointed look as I brought my coffee through from the kitchen. Who were you expecting then, Mademoiselle? Hugh Grant, with his debonair charm and luxuriant locks? Well, *désolé*, you'll have to settle for me!

Naturally, when I sat down on the sofa, I made sure I left a respectable distance between us. She had already got out the text book: a schoolbook for pity's sake. Back to the classroom at 52! Then she launched straight in:

Unit 1, page 1. La France – full-page map of her homeland, which she indicated with her chewed fingernail.

'Qu'est-ce que c'est?'

'La France… naturellement, Danielle.'

'Oui. Mais il existe un autre nom.'

Another name. Surely I must know another name for France? Look at the shape… Apart from a flattened starfish, inspiration deserted me. Danielle's chestnut brown eyes were waiting.

'Ça s'appelle l'Hexagone. Vous comprenez?'

'Ah, oui, l'Hexagone. C'est fascinant, Danielle.'

And it was fascinating, one of the highlights of our session, l'Hexagone. After that we went overseas : les Départements d'Outre-Mer, les Territoires d'Outre-Mer. When she turned to the colour photograph of an idyllic palm beach on Guadeloupe, I tried my best to sound enthusiastic.

'Ah, c'est fantastique. Une islande tropicale!'

'Une île. Not islande.'

'Pardon. Une île. Avec la plage exotique. Idéal pour les vacances.'

'Ça dépend,' she shrugged.

Not her thing apparently, tropical holidays. Still, after that came my chance to shine in reading aloud. An entire page devoted to the French regions and départements. To her credit, she listened attentively, managing not to show too much disdain for my pronunciation, apart from the word *développement*. She repeated it in her heavy monotone and I thought I'd got it well enough but each time she dismissed my evidently feeble attempt with a resounding 'non'.

What next? Oh yes, the mind-numbing geographical crossword. She sat adjusting her hairband while I pencilled in what I could, starting with Pas de Calais. I remember she seemed distinctly ill at ease, on account of her oily skin problems, presumably, or was she bored? Whatever the case, she was hardly inspiring company.

I suppose our final chat was mildly diverting. First up, the weather. 'Le soleil brille et le ciel est bleu,' I said. 'Bien,' she said. Did I detect she was warming to me slightly? Then we reached the dizzy heights of climate. And, as she was keen to point out, 'le climat est plus agréable en France'. Likewise *la gastronomie, la patisserie, l'architecture, les transports publics, le système scolaire, la philosophie, le ski*. Yes, who would disagree? It is all so much better in France. But, refusing to let her defeat me, I found myself spouting the old mantra.

'Mais Danielle, en Angleterre nous avons le National Health Service. C'est unique, c'est equitable.'

Oh, her look of disbelief:

'Mais non! Les hôpitaux en Angleterre sont dangereux. Ce n'est pas comme ça en France. Non, en France les hôpitaux sont modernes et propres. Mais en Angleterre vous avez ce problème scandaleux. Les microbes, cette chose à résistances multiples... SARM... You say MRSA?'

She had a point, too. Give me half a chance and I'd be tempted to escape the NHS and defect to clean, efficient

French hospitals any day. Or possibly retrain and set up as a GP in a nice quiet pocket of Provence, where the ex-pats would be only too pleased to bring their ailments to Doctor Mike.

At a minute to eleven, she began stowing the text book away in her rucksack, looking tired. Poor girl – I think she suffered more than me during our rather awkward hour together. I thanked her of course and handed her the crisp note.

'By the way, which part of France are you from?' I thought I'd make some effort as I showed her out.

'Mulhouse.'

'Moulouse? Where's that?'

She paused by the weeping fig in the hallway, scrutinising the passably glossy foliage, which was evidently far more interesting than my face.

'Near to the Swiss border. Département Haut Rhin... in Alsace.'

'Ah, Alsace. Interesting wines... Vous aimez le vin, Danielle?'

'Non, pas spécialement.'

Oh come on, lighten up you leaden lump! There must be something that makes you tick.

'Et vous préférez?'

'Le Coca-Cola. Et le weekend' – sudden glimmer of a smile – 'j'aime bien aller au pub... Pour les cocktails.'

'Ah, c'est très intéressant. Merci, Danielle. Au revoir.'

And off she went, the monosyllabic *Alsacienne*. We said nothing about another session. No point – I might as well have sat down with the book by myself, set the timer and looked up the answers at the back. Dispense with the tutor all together and buy a decent bottle with the proceeds.

So back to the drawing board. But already we had crossed the magical threshold from June into July and the various language agencies seemed dead – deserted no doubt by their staff heading back across the Channel for *les grandes vacances*. Eventually a gravel-voiced female from the fourth agency picked up the phone and offered me something: how about signing up for ten weekly sessions starting late September? One of their best tutors, naturally: young, arty, Sorbonne graduate by the name of André-Pierre. *Très cultivé*, by all accounts. Well, yes… perhaps a little too *cultivé* for me.

It was hopeless – enough to make me even contemplate joining an evening class come September. After all, why pay good money for the miserable Danielle to grunt and turn the page for me? And why shell out in advance for the precious André-Pierre to put in an appearance two months after he was needed? Why indeed? But then again, why on earth would anyone consider paying sixty quid an hour to a bloody-minded French female with delusions of grandeur and one hell of an attitude problem? Yes, why indeed?

'Allo… Héllo?'

'Madame Lorance? It's Michael Westover.'

'Yes.'

'Madame, I take it you recall our conversation the other week re private lessons?'

'Yes. I remember it. You were going to contact some other language tutors, yes?' Cool. Nonchalant. But not impolite.

'Indeed. I got in touch with several. In fact one was able to see me very promptly. Very reasonable charges, too.'

'Good, I am glad they can help you.'

'Ah, well, let's say the service wasn't *entirely* satisfactory. So, just for the record, would you mind clarifying your rate again?'

'Un instant.' I had caught her on the back foot. 'Alors, tarif professionnel, it's as we said, sixty pounds for one hour.'

'How about fifty?'

'*O quelle audace!* You try to barter with me?'

'Well, naturally, as a doctor, I'm used to looking at both sides of the equation – the patient's viewpoint, our viewpoint – and, wherever possible, proposing solutions. Compromises if you like.'

'Compromise? I don't need your…'

'Look, if it helps, I'm willing to pay in advance. How about five sessions for starters?'

'Five! But Docteur Westover, I thought you understood I am very busy. You realise it is already six July and the 'olidays …'

'I appreciate you're in demand but I'm sure you'll do your best to squeeze me in.'

'But really, I…'

'Go on! See what you can do.'

I caught the sigh at the other end of the line, followed by the more hassled tone of voice.

'Ecoutez, c'est difficile, c'est très difficile… Je vais réfléchir. Une minute.'

Ah yes, that glorious interlude when the receiver went down followed by distant, muffled sounds: a drawer being pulled out, a dramatic sigh, some loud tutting. The hasty leafing through of diary pages, then more tutting and exasperated sighing. She left me hanging on for a good minute before coming back, sounding distinctly *agitée*.

'Alors, voyons, nous sommes le 6 juillet. Et je pars bientôt en vacances. C'est impossible, je suis vraiment débordée en ce moment. Tous ces clients… Débordée! Let me explain…'

'No need. You're going away on holiday soon and you're up to your eyes with clients. I take it that's the meaning of *débordé*?'

'Well, *débordé*, it means very busy, overflowing with work. Just like the rivers are overflowing in the floods. But how did you say in English – over your eyes?'

'Up to your eyes. Well, in the first person you'd say: I'm up to *my* eyes.'

'Up to my eyes... Yes, I like this expression very much.'

'Good.' Delighted to be of assistance to you in perfecting your English, Madame. Free of charge, too...

'I suppose ac-tu-al-ly your French comprehension is quite good, isn't it?'

'Thanks... Yes, a little more coaching and, who knows, I might speak quite decent French. Then I'll be able to think seriously about moving over and settling in la belle France. Still, thanks for your time – I'll keep looking.'

Perhaps it was the pathos. Either that or my game of bluff had its effect.

'One moment please.'

Another silence, but shorter this time; promising enough for me to pick up my pen and go so far as to remove its lid.

'So Docteur Westover... You live in Putnay, don't you? And in fact I live in Wimbledon. So we are very close, yes?'

'Indeed.'

'OK, d'accord. I will offer you one lesson. After that, we will see. *On verra*, as we say. So when are you free?'

'Oh I'm pretty flexible at the moment. Daytime, evenings – I can adjust my diary to suit you.'

'But you are working in the hospital...'

'Actually I'm taking a career break, a kind of sabbatical.'

'Une année sabbatique?'

I remember the puzzled note in her voice and, leaning back in my leather recliner, again I tried to picture the face at the end of the line.

'Oui, Madame. Exactement.' We left it at that. No point in trying to explain the English concept of gardening leave.

'So, Docteur Westover, I can see you next week, thirteenth July. Seven o'clock. But just one hour.'

'Seven o'clock on the thirteenth… suits me fine! That's very good of you, Madame.'

'Et votre adresse?'

'Numéro un…' – I tried to do it in French until the ridiculousness struck me – 'Number 1, Monterey Drive, as in Monterey, California.'

I remember, as we sorted out precise directions, allowing myself a second to bask in the delicious satisfaction of having hooked the elusive Violette! But of course I had to sound cool and matter-of-fact, just as I would with a difficult patient.

'So I'll see you at seven on the thirteenth of July. Our development's tucked away in a side road off the Heath – you'll see some tall pines at the end of the road. When you get to the gates, press apartment one. You can park in the space, first left, adjacent to my car, black metallic…'

'All right. And Docteur Westover, I trust you can provide us with a suitable working environment. It must be quiet and uncluttered – and with good *acoustique*.'

Naturellement, Madame. Naturellement.

CHAPTER 2

We met on the thirteenth of July – one day short of Bastille Day. Of course, it would have been neat to have had our first meeting on *le quatorze juillet* – to be engaged in our introductory tête à tête while, across the Channel, thousands of fireworks were bursting into the evening sky. But the thirteenth it was, allowing me a clear seven days to prepare.

So the cleaners came on the previous day to give the place a thorough going-over – hoovered, polished, urology journals stowed away. Everything just so for Madame. And on the day I booked myself in for a spruce-up at the barber's: a number two with the clippers that instantly toned down the receding patches, followed by the grooming package. That put a spring into my step on the way back up the Putney High Street.

It was a scorcher as I remember, 28°C or so, and after stopping off at the pub for a sandwich, I returned home, passing through the open gates, noting that the automatic system still hadn't been fixed. After that I managed a little cosmetic gardening – dead-heading the sun-blasted roses and tying the riotous red clematis onto the obelisque by the path. Then I took it upon myself to wash the Porsche. Classic diversion activity, of course, but very satisfying, shining up the basalt black. By late afternoon everything was pristine: sparkling *Carrera*, sparkling home and – duly showered – sparkling me. And still time to rehearse some scintillating French: Bonsoir Madame. Entrez... Vous désirez le café ou le thé? Avec du lait? Avec sucre?

I don't think I went to such lengths during my youth, not even when I was wooing Moira. But then, admittedly, never before have I prepared for the arrival of a *maîtresse*. After all the preparations, I remember making an omelette, pouring a glass of Merlot and waiting. Yet somehow time seemed to hang still in the air, like a roller coaster poised at the top of the incline.

Luke rang at about six forty-five – sure knows how to pick his moment. Just to let me know he would be staying up in Leeds with Rachel until the end of July. Well, of course he would, lucky lad. I would have done the same in his position except I didn't have a steady girlfriend at nineteen. No, we were three male medics in digs – car-less, mobile-less, penniless but surviving pretty well on spag bol, baked beans and frankfurters and cheap lager, while mugging up on Gray's Anatomy to the constant backdrop of the Stones, Hendrix, Free... that is, when we weren't planting bits of intestine in each other's pockets!

Of course, I knew the reason for the call; he was burning with curiosity after receiving my text.

'So, what's she like, your French teacher?'

'Oh, Brigitte Bardot probably. How should I know? I've only got a voice to go on. But she sounded fairly young.'

'Compared to you!'

'Very funny. But I admit voices can be deceptive. You know, Luke, I've had some prospective patients ring me up and they sound youthful, flirtatious even, but when they present in clinic, they turn out to be late fifties. Still, as for Violette, all will be revealed.'

'Violet! What sort of a name is that?'

'Oh come on! Sounds quite pretty and cute to me.'

'You reckon? And that's what you're excited about? Some middle-aged woman who's got a name like an old granny?'

Then he called me sad!

I began looking out at ten to seven; eager to see the enigma crystallise in the flesh. And what exactly was I expecting? It is hard to cast my mind back, even half a year ago. I suppose I had formed a sketchy mental picture based on a few minutes over the phone: She would be early thirties, brunette, tanned, slim, well dressed. A whiff of perfume and a whiff of cigarettes. Also, I expected an air of self-assurance – red lipstick and dark eyes with a feisty glint. As for the car, a little red sports or cabriolet. That's what she would arrive in. If she arrived at all.

But no – about two minutes to seven, a dark saloon rolled in through the gates. Volvo, basic model, several years old. Quite impossible to see the driver from my angle on the first floor. The car swept round over the gravel and reversed, surprisingly slickly, into the space by my *Carrera*. Then as the driver's door opened – *le moment de la vérité*. And that first impression bore little resemblance to the fantasy image that had been floating in my mind's eye and, in hindsight, little resemblance to the reality of the woman I have since come to know.

Yes, you were an extraordinary vision on that summer evening, Violette. Not so much mistress as headmistress with that voluminous, long grey suit, the pinned-up hair and the executive case. The efficient twist of the wrist as you locked the car, the purposeful stride to my front door.

'Bonsoir, Madame.'

'Bonsoir, docteur. Enchantée.'

A cool outstretched hand and a restrained smile. Light eyes that met mine for a second and then looked down.

'Enchanté, Madame. Entrez.'

'Merci.'

She was in. In my hallway, all prim and proper and buttoned up! Some *maîtresse*, I remember thinking; one with a penchant for tasteful suits! Age-wise, she could have been anything from mid-forties, wearing well, to thirty-something with a surprisingly mature taste in clothing. There was a hint of awkwardness between us, perhaps each of us remembering the edgy phone call.

'Well, all the living accommodation is upstairs, so if you'd like to come this way…'

So there I was, a couple of treads behind, taking in all the details: light brown hair, with a few sunstreaks, tightly slicked back and pinned up into a twist. Nice perfume. Average height and smallish build, although it was hard to gauge size under all that material. Yes, that ludicrously long skirt, trailing on the stairs ahead of me, prompting me to hazard my joke about breaking a leg.

She paused by the side window.

'You are so lucky to have those trees. I saw them immediately when I turned into the road, as you said.'

'Superb, aren't they? Monterey pines, so the groundsman informs me.'

'Ah, so this explains Monterey Drive!' OK, so it was small talk but a hundred per cent improvement on the grunting Danielle. 'And look – you even have a cedar tree!'

'Yes, that tree has to be at least a hundred years old – a survivor from the original house here. Now let me guess the French: un cédar de Lebanon?'

'Un cèdre du Liban.' Such poetic words, spoken softly.

'Ah, cèdre du Liban.'

I realise now that during the exchange there was no eye contact. Despite the pleasantries, she seemed a distant, wary creature, gazing out at the trees, and not looking towards me at all. It struck me she was surprisingly light-skinned for a French national; a pale woodland violet, as I said inwardly to myself!

Truth be told, she didn't strike me as stunningly pretty but quietly attractive with a sculpted, Continental bone structure.

The dining room was still like a greenhouse after the blazing day. But trust Madame to decline my offer of hanging up her jacket.

'Thank you but it's very cool, being made of linen, from Ireland in fact.'

'Ah, I see.'

So, cool, expensive Irish linen, yards and yards of it... She was standing in the middle of the room, looking a little uncertain.

'Please take a seat at the table, whichever side you like... although you get a better view from the right.'

'Yes, why not? I can see the *parterre* with the flowers.'

She put her case on the table and no doubt I stood, watching like some fascinated schoolboy: what exactly would a *maîtresse* have inside her attaché case? A clipboard with a sheet of lined A4. Some photocopied text. A bundle of postcards. Not forgetting the bilingual dictionary that she put gently down onto the oak table. All very reasonable and respectable.

'Vous désirez le thé, Madame? Le café? Ou le vin?'

'Avez-vous de l'eau minérale?'

'Oui... Perrier?'

'Très bien.'

By the time I returned from the kitchen with our water, ice and lemon, two new items had appeared on the dining table: that iridescent fountain pen, shiny as a beetle, and, positioned parallel to it, the compact, silver mobile phone. I took my glass over to my side of the table and then, just after seven, we started.

'So, we meet at last. Finalement!'

Yes, I had to open with a platitude. Still, there we were, finally embarking on our teacher-student relationship.

'Alors, docteur' – confident, businesslike smile – 'We will start with introducing ourselves. Name, nationality, where we live, and our profession. I will begin. Je m'appelle Violette Lorance. Je suis française. J'habite Wimbledon. Je suis professeur de français. Et vous?'

'Je m'appelle Michael Westover. Je suis anglais. J'habite Londres, à Putney. Je suis urologiste.'

'Urologue, we say. Try it.'

'Urologue.'

'Not bad but you sound too English. Say it the French way, like this: rrr… rrr.' Purring like a cat, she was! 'You see? Very soft and low in your throat.'

'Je suis yurrologue.'

'Excellent.'

Madame looked pleased. Suddenly she raised her index finger.

'Listen. Ecoutez! I have been living in London since five years. In French, I say: J'habite Londres depuis cinq ans.'

Well, well, Madame, I thought, wonder what brought you to our shores five years ago? And did you come alone or perhaps with Monsieur Lorance? And how come, in the three years I've lived here, our paths have not crossed – not in the High Street, on the tube, on Wimbledon Common, at the checkout? But then, on reflection, why should we have met, being just two of thousands?

'Et vous, Docteur Westover, vous habitez Putnay depuis combien de temps?'

'Je habitay à Putney depuis trois ans.'

Immediately her hand darted to the iridescent pen and I saw her make a note on her clipboard. 'Now did you notice what you just said?' Slight overtones of the schoolmistress.

'No, what did I say?'

'Je habitay! So many of my English students make this mistake: je habitay, je preferay…'

'Ah. I meant to say: j'habite!'

'OK, d'accord. Et bien, Docteur Westover, vous avez un grand appartement!'

'Oui, c'est un duplex, Madame.'

'Ah oui, un duplex. So there is another floor upstairs?'

'Yes.'

'Et vous trouvez que c'est pratique?'

'You're asking if I find it practical?'

'Mm.'

'Oui, très pratique. Mon duplex est grand, moderne, confortable. Avec quatre chambres… Madame, vous désirez le tour de mon duplex?'

The idea just popped into my head so I threw it in for good measure. And to my surprise, she accepted. But, even more surprising, as we were getting up from our chairs for the grand tour, I caught her hesitating, looking down at the mobile on the table.

'Expecting a call?'

'No, I just keep it with me as a kind of *sécurité*.'

'Ah yes, a sensible precaution although sometimes it takes more than a mobile to protect oneself.'

That earned me a sharp look.

'Well, for your information, docteur, I always prepare an emergency text – just as a precaution, of course.' Teasing little smile.

'Of course! But who would you send it to, if I may ask?'

She looked at me as if I were an idiot.

'But to the police, natur-al-ly! The text has all the necessary information: the client's name, address, the date, the time. I just press the button and – hop. *Voilà!*'

Ingenious! But somewhat alarming to think she had all my details keyed in as a potential kidnapper or sex maniac before ever setting eyes on me.

'That's brilliant! Ha ha…' It was a stupid, nervous laugh of mine and no doubt I looked and sounded all the more suspicious to her. 'Still,' I said, 'you can trust me; I'm a doctor.' That old cliché! She said nothing but gave me a slightly pained look while slipping the mobile into her pocket.

We started in the living room and straightaway she commented on the black leather suite: 'Style typiquement masculin'. Then she was drawn to the balcony and I caught snippets of French to do with the agreeable view and the verdant garden. When she turned back, we had our memorable conversation about the Manet print.

'Ah, this painting: *Au bar des Folies-Bergères*.'

'Yes, very evocative with all the spectators and the smoke. Captures the atmosphere perfectly, doesn't it?'

'Oh yes. I like it very much. For example, the way he painted the oranges, the champagne bottle… and how you say … the pretty bar girl, yes?'

I caught her looking at me with a glint in her eye.

'Hm, yes, she has a certain charm. But what really intrigues me is this curious reflection. In fact, is there a mirror at all? What do you think?'

'Oh, it's a mirror, definitely.' She stepped back from the picture, frowning slightly. 'But no, ac-tu-al-ly it does not work. The reflection is in the wrong place.'

'Exactly. Very strange… and equally bizarre, see those two green dashes in the top corner? What do you think they are?'

Screwed up eyes, a slight shrug: 'Maybe they are lamps – am I right?'

'No, not lamps. Legs!'

'*Legs*?' Wide-eyed astonishment!

'Yes, legs. You see, you're looking at the green ankle boots belonging to a trapeze artist! No, seriously, those are her calves, disappearing off the top edge of the picture.'

Delicious little gasp of surprise. 'Yes, yes… I never saw it before. So crazy, these little legs in the corner – just the *bottines* with no body!' Then she smiled. A surprisingly generous, carefee smile that lit up her face and made her look younger and, it must be said: prettier.

After that, we did the kitchen. Evidently all the gleaming stainless steel made a good impression, likewise the range. But the item of greatest interest was immediately obvious.

'Mais ce réfrigerateur, c'est énorme… 2 mètres!'

Naturally, I was only too pleased to reveal the precious bottles, relishing her surprise.

'Oh les vins! Et les vins de qualité – Chablis, Pouilly Fumé, Sancerre… C'est votre passion, docteur?'

'Oui, Madame. Et vous, vous aimez…?'

'Moi, je préfère le champagne.'

I could tell that from the delight on her face.

After the kitchen we went upstairs, Madame first, hitching up her long grey skirt. Which is when I noticed *the shoes*. Black patent with high heels – FMs, no less! An unusual choice with her traditional suit – but then again, not so surprising for a woman calling herself la Maîtresse.

The studio was a mess with all the wood shavings on the floor. Strictly out of bounds to the cleaners, I hadn't counted on showing it off to visitors. So we merely glanced in before moving on to Luke's room. I pointed out the photo of him, fifteen or so, on the drums in our conservatory at Waterford Road. Told her he was now a strapping, slightly surly nineteen-year-old doing maths at Leeds. Then she noticed the shot of the three of us at Arles, all happy families, posing outside the arena. Moira, raven-haired and stunning, grabbing my pubescent son's arm in a rare relaxed moment.

'C'est Luke avec 13 ans. Et c'est moi... Et c'est Moira, ma femme. Non, ex-femme... Nous sommes divorcés.'

She gave me a sympathetic look.

'Ah, le divorce. C'est difficile, ça.'

'Oui, très difficile... Et vous Violette, vous êtes mariée?'

Several seconds of frosty silence followed by a sharp, challenging look.

'C'est *moi* qui pose les questions!'

'Excusez-moi.'

Touchy. Very, very touchy. In near silence, we bypassed the gleaming bathroom for the study, where the cleaners had tidied up the medical dictionaries and journals on the shelves. She nodded. Then my bedroom – immaculately made bed, fresh air coming in from the balcony...

'Ma chambre, Madame.'

'Ah oui.'

But she seemed distinctly underwhelmed, possibly a little uncomfortable, and so we headed back downstairs to the first floor. She took her place again at the dining table, still looking slightly tense. So, thinking I would put her mind at rest, I took out my cheque book and wrote her a hefty sum, after which we pencilled several dates in our diaries. But I noticed, as she put her cheque away, the ominous frown.

'Docteur Westover.'

'Yes?'

'During our lessons, I prefer you to call me Madame. You see, all my Englishmen, they call me Madame: 'oui, Madame' 'non, Madame', 'certainement Madame'. But never Violette.'

'No problem. I'll stick to Madame.'

'Good. And I will call you Docteur Westover?'

'Well, strictly speaking, it should be Mister Westover. But let's say Mike... or Michel, if you like.'

'Yes, Michel is perfect.'

After that, we talked about her postcards of France, comparing notes on the places we had visited. It was quite satisfying, la Maîtresse speaking her beautiful, clear French while I was pushing myself to keep up the flow of conversation.

'Vous avez visité Paris, sans doute, Michel?'

'Ah oui, Notre Dame, Louvre, Versailles...'

Then there was the unmistakable arched gallery and sheet of water of the Château de Chenonceau. Followed by Chamonix with Mont Blanc rising up behind. But she said she was no skier. What else? The grandeur of Bordeaux, Dijon, Nice...

We spent a while on her picture of the market at Aix-en-Provence: *les abricots, les grosses tomates, les olives...* The Jerusalem artichokes she called *topinambours*. ('Try it Michel: top-een-um-boor...') Then those beautiful white peaches. I remember her nodding 'mm, mm' as I despaired of the tasteless bullets in our supermarkets that bear no resemblance to their succulent French cousins. The ice seemed to be thawing a little; in fact, I remember around that time she undid a couple of her jacket buttons.

What else? Ah, how could I forget: Grasse. 'Oh, Michel, l'odeur, l'odeur...' She swooned exactly like Moira! Memories of us spending the entire morning there, my ex-wife disappearing into the various *parfumeries* and emerging with a lifetime's worth of perfume and soap, while Luke and I were kicking our heels, dying to escape the heavily scented streets and breathe fresh, salty air instead. Grasse led on nicely to her postcard of the Gorges du Verdon and our reminiscences of the exhilarating drive up to the viewpoints and the dizzying view down to the turquoise river below.

It was noticeable how she opened up with those pictures, sharing the delights of her childhood visits to her great-uncle's house in the Rhône Valley. In fact, suddenly she seemed to be talking to me as if I were a friend rather than a student.

'Oh, Michel, le nougat tendre… My grand-uncle, he made it from almonds and the honay from the bee hives in his garden…and it was so marvellously delicious. *Onctueux*, we say. My brother and I, we loved it!' She smiled across, swirling the lemon slice in the glass. 'You must try it one day.'

Finally came the flurry of postcards on Monet's garden, Deauville, Rouen cathedral, picturesque Honfleur.

'You seem to have a thing for Normandy!'

'But of course!' Her eyes danced. 'It is my region.'

So that explains it, I remember thinking. You're a Normandy lass, hence the light eyes and the lack of olive skin, and the clear, unhurried way of speaking. She was obviously proud of her region, extolling its scenic variety: the pastures, the patchwork effect of the *bocage*, historic Rouen, the glamour of Deauville, the wildness of la Hague west of Cherbourg…

'Ah oui, Madame, c'est intéressant.'

'Oui, mais la gloire de Normandie…' – triumphant look as she flashed her trump card – 'c'est le Mont-Saint-Michel! Vous avez visité?'

'Non, jamais.'

'Oh, il faut absolument aller le voir! You must go to see it one day, it is extraordinary.'

She then went into raptures about its magical effect from a distance, *magnifique en silhouette*… And with a smile she said how all Normandy residents were fortunate that this jewel of France happened to sit just their side of the boundary with

Brittany. She was speaking with authority, as if she owned the Mont-Saint-Michel – but then, I suppose, she can rightfully consider it hers, being a mere stone's throw from the town in which she was born. Avranches. Of course, I didn't let on that I'd never heard of the place.

It was at this point in the conversation, clearly relaxed, that she decided, with a sleek movement of her shoulders, to shed her linen jacket altogether and, in the process, treat me to an unexpectedly lovely vision: a very shapely, toned little figure in a close-fitting, black sleeveless top. *Très chic… Très français…*

Now, had we had a nice bottle of Provence rosé in front of us, we might have happily passed the evening, exchanging tales of the delights of France. But all good things come to an end. She bundled up the postcards and we began the final exercise on Strasbourg, which was to be the cause of my undoing.

It started well enough. She handed me the photocopy of the tourist brochure and listened while I read aloud. After some trouble pronouncing *'Une ville d'ambiguïtés'* we did the whistle-stop tour of the city: la cathédrale mediévale, le Conseil de l'Europe, les tramways, La Petite France – at which point Madame chose to take a diversion, in English, to fill me in on her favourite part of the city.

'Yes, la Petite France, this is a charming part of Strasbourg. You can walk by the old houses next to the waterways along the streets they call *les quais*… Quai des Pêcheurs, Quai des Bateliers… It is very nice and peaceful, especially in spring, when the green willow trees are cascading over the water.'

'Sounds very pleasant. You seem to know it well…' (Sailing close to the wind with my attempt to elicit information from the guarded Violette! But this time, curiously, she was quite forthcoming.)

'Oh, yes I used to visit there quite a few years ago. And this one thing I remember especially: we were walking in the Parc de l'Orangerie, close to the Council of Europe, and we heard this strange noise from a tree: tak tak tak. So we looked up and there is this enormous bird on an enormous nest. Well, my friend instantly knew its name: *Cigogne blanche*.'

'Your friend was good at ornithology.'

'Yes. Anyway, this bird, I forget the English name, but you know – the bird of folklore that brings the children.'

'You mean a stork!'

'Yes, exactly. Imagine this, a stork on its nest, so near to all the European representatives in their limousines.'

'Extraordinary.'

'Yes, it was… it was…'

For a moment she looked quite distant, lost in her memories of Strasbourg – or possibly of her mysterious friend? Anyway, she soon broke out of her reverie and glanced at the time.

'So, Michel, to finish our text, please read about the delicious Alsace food and the wine bars.'

'Avec plaisir, Madame.'

It seemed perfectly simple as I read it aloud; a run-down of the local wines on offer in the Strasbourg *wynstub* (Riesling, Sylvaner, Gewurztraminer…), the damson and blueberry tarts in the patisseries, and the *choucroute aux saucisses* and savoury *tartes flambées* served in the restaurants. She smiled and said my comprehension was good and I had a nice, rich voice, ideal for speaking French. Naturally, I was beginning to feel quite satisfied with my performance, not to say a little flattered, until she flagged up a pronunciation problem on the very last word.

'Would you repeat the last sentence, Michel, about finding a small, cosy restaurant.'

'Pour savourer les spécialités de la cuisine alsacienne, cherchez un bon petit restaurant intime.'

'Yes, you did it again, just on the word intimate...' Little smile to put me at my ease. 'You see, for our word *intime*, you don't say *in*-teem; you say *an*-teem. So we say: un petit restaurant *an-teem.*'

'Oh really?' Something niggled in me and I felt sure of my ground. 'But I thought it would be *in*-teem. As in *in*évitable.'

'No, that's different. Let me try to explain the principle. The pronunciation depends if we have a consonant or a vowel coming after the *in.*'

'I see.'

'But if you find it confusing, Michel, just accept what I say.'

'OK then, I'll take your word for it...'

That really got to her. I hadn't intended the words to sound pompous but evidently they hit a raw nerve. She looked and sounded *agitée*.

'Docteur Westover, I realise as a member of the medical profession it is hard for you to accept that you could ever be mistaken but...'

'Look, I was merely questioning...'

'I see – well, perhaps it would be prudent to wait a little longer before you challenge my knowledge of my maternal language!'

I can hear that tone now – haughty, sarcastic and very French.

'Look, please don't take offence.'

'Oh, I am not offended. I am disappointed.' Dramatic sigh as she clicked open her executive case and began stowing away her A4 pad and postcards, glancing up occasionally. 'Disappointed that I agree to come to teach you French, and this evening we were having a nice, cultured conversation together, but suddenly you do not respect my authority *in my own language!* So – you need to prove it to yourself. Look in the dictionary. Find the word *intime.*'

That feisty glare as she pushed her dictionary towards me across the table! She had gone extremely pale and tight-lipped, and her chest was rising and falling rapidly in her little black top. Prone to hyperventilation, I thought.

Small print dancing before my eyes:

Intestin… Intestinal… Intimation… Intime.

'Have you found it?'

Suddenly there she was, la Maîtresse, on my side of the table, wearing little gold reading glasses, looking very schoolmistressy.

'Yes, look: there.' Leaning over me now, surprisingly close. 'Now: look at the phonetic transcription in the square brackets, which tells us how to pronounce the word. Notice, Michel, the Greek letter E with the little mark on top like a wave on the sea. You see it?'

Concentrate! For Pete's sake don't be sidetracked by the proximity of her smooth, toned arm virtually brushing my cheek…

'Yes.'

'This sign tells us to produce the same nasal *an* sound we make in the word *vin* – and you English have certainly no difficulty to pronounce that one.'

'No.'

'So you will accept that the dictionary, it does not lie.'

'Indeed.'

'Therefore now you will believe what I say to you, yes?'

Wonderful old-fashioned look delivered through the oval spectacles.

'Yes. And I apologise if…'

'Good. I accept your apology.' She straightened up, stepped away from my side and with a smooth gesture removed her glasses. And when she spoke, the agitation had left her voice.

'So, Michel, to finish our lesson and reinforce the principle, I want to consider some other French words beginning with *in*-followed by a consonant. Can you think of one?'

'*Intelligent* – which I imagine would be pronounced *antelligent*.'

'That's right, exactly. Any more? Try writing them down on your piece of paper.'

She went over to the window, looking out while I was thinking of my simple phrases, to the sound of the clock ticking away. After a minute or so she came back to my side to check what I'd written, asking me to read aloud:

Un film intéressant.
Un journaliste intelligent.
L'univers infini.

'Good, Michel.' An approving smile. 'Now I know you will remember this lesson in pronunciation.'

'I certainly will.'

'And most of all, you will never forget your old friend.'

'Old friend?'

'Well, of course, I am talking about that little word for being intimate... in French...'

Long, inviting pause, hanging in the air... and I glanced up to find beautiful, grey-green eyes looking softly but intently into mine. Then her lips parted as she spoke that magical little word.

'*Intime*...'

'Ah, yes...'

Holding my gaze a fraction longer...

'Never forget it, Michel... *intime*.'

CHAPTER 3

I finished Hole-in-the-Head that night – at around three a.m.
Not that woodcarving had been on my agenda; my intention
was merely to round off the evening with a leisurely stroll on
Putney Heath, and possibly pop in for a pint. By nine o'clock
the heat had dissipated but it was still mild and balmy, drawing
out the resinous smell of the pines as I walked out through the
gates. For a moment it could have been the south of France.

People were lingering outside the Telegraph but otherwise,
bar one dog-walker, I had the heath to myself. I couldn't have
picked a better evening for a walk; rosy sky, the sound of swifts
and even a pair of bats patrolling for insects around the trees.
Shortly afterwards, I almost stepped on that male stag beetle
lumbering along on the pavement. Extraordinary thing,
struggling to hold up its awesome set of mandibles. The first
I've seen since Edward and I found one in our youth.

After the heath, resisting the temptation of the pub, I took
the side roads, passing the solid Edwardian houses, some with
lights on and curtains open. Occasional wafts of barbecue,
alternating with the scent of flowering limes. Now and then, as
I wandered, a linguistic gem would glint at the back of my
mind. *Cèdre du Liban… Le nougat onctueux…* I'd learnt some
interesting vocabulary with the mysterious Violette.

Striking was the word that came to mind; striking, rather
than beautiful. Although there was a certain attractiveness
about her, especially when the serious façade dropped for a

moment. While under those layers of grey linen, in her close-fitting black top, there was perhaps a hint of flirtatiousness. But she was not the Parisian sex bomb of a *maîtresse* I had imagined from the advert. Something was missing. Basically, I suppose you would call it the 'wow' factor.

Now with Moira, there was instant wow. Two minutes in her company at the graduation ball and I had her sussed – not only as an absolute stunner, but also as prime candidate for the potential role of doctor's wife. Well, back then it all seemed perfectly obvious to me: jet-black hair, expensive red dress, witty, intelligent, dripping with self-assurance and easy Irish charm, she was one highly desirable package – and everyone knew it.

Whereas with Violette, nothing was clear-cut; instead there was depth and mystery. Take nationality: while clearly not English, one could hardly say she looked classically French; more Swiss or Belgian, or even eastern European, you might have thought. And unlike Moira – so keen to tell me about her sisters and her brilliant, entrepreneurial Daddy – Violette evidently decided to keep her family background firmly under wraps and maintain secrecy. Not that you could label her a shy, shrinking violet, given her capacity to dole out the odd rebuke or sharp look! Yes, that was the fascinating thing: the extraordinary mixture. Thinking back over our first hour, didn't she exhibit a bit of everything? Guardedness and – when she wanted it – openness; seriousness and informality; a scholarly objectivity interspersed with warm encouragement; and a hint of flirtatiousness offset with the occasional blast of *froideur*.

In other words, the woman was a living, breathing, walking bundle of contradictions! Take the way she presented herself, clothed from neck to ankle, only, at a moment of her choosing, to reveal her stunning little figure with fabulous *sang-froid*. And her bizarre initial wariness of men… the spiel about the emergency text message; her pains to establish the correct distance between us across the table; her use of sufficient but not excessive eye contact during the first fifty-five minutes – oh yes, all highly laudable and professional. Except then: *voilà* Madame, leaning over me, her fingertip touching mine in the dictionary, her bare arm virtually brushing my cheek!

Then there was the way she emphasised that word *intime* so dramatically. I remember her soft voice replaying in my head as I came back over the heath in the fading light. She lowered her pitch as she spoke, drawing out the sound of the 'm' in a soft whisper: *an-teeem-m*… And all the while she was gazing at me with her grey-green eyes, like a cat.

It must have been around half past ten when I approached Monterey Drive. First priority: up to the study, to hunt out my trusty book of British insects, vintage 1969, tattered jacket and all. Inside – the cast of six-legged characters, winged and wingless, still strangely familiar after all these years. Springtails, mayflies, dragonflies, crickets… and towards the back, there was the illustration that used to fascinate me as a kid: two male stag beetles locked in combat with their antler-like jaws. *Lucanus cervus* it said; strong fliers, seen on fine evenings from May to August in southern England. After that, I couldn't resist a look at the butterflies and moths. All those wonderful names from the past: Clouded Yellow, Grizzled Skipper, Garden Tiger, Oak Eggar and the one with the mottled green wings whose name my brother and I could never pronounce, let alone understand: *Merveille du Jour.*

I e-mailed Edward there and then about the stag beetle – little test of his memory. Then, since my mind was still buzzing, I armed myself with a chilled Stella and headed up to the studio, to find my good friend Hole-in-the-Head waiting by the sheets of glasspaper on the workbench – looking suitably quirky and artistic in the white ash, like an elongated broad bean with the asymmetric orifice I'd drilled into it during a 'Henry Moore' episode. Having almost completed the chiselling and filing last time, all that remained was a couple of hours of sanding and finishing; the ideal thing for an over-stimulated mind that refused to lie down.

Time passed rapidly against the backdrop of Pink Floyd; the last honing with the riffler file, working reasonably well with my left hand. A swig or two of lager and then the sanding. As I got into the rhythm, those proverbial words came back to me from school assemblies: '...always remembering, it is not the beginning of the task but the continuation of the same until it be thoroughly finished that yieldeth the true glory'. Ah yes, to see a task through from start to finish – there is much satisfaction to be gained from that, whether in theatre or in the workshop. And I was feeling buoyant as the realisation came to me; finally, after weeks and weeks of disinterest, I was inspired to pick up the chisel and finish my labour of love.

While my hands were engaged in their task, I remember my mind was setting the world to rights. Starting with the scarcity of butterflies and moths these days. Are pesticides to blame or simply too many wet English summers? Or perhaps if Edward and I hadn't been so zealous in asphyxiating them and sticking a pin through the thorax, there would be more of them flying around now!

Then, as I recall, came thoughts of meltdown in the markets and meltdown in the Arctic... and then Californian bushfires and parched Australian farmlands, and reporters roaming the planet, bandying about the term 'carbon footprint' at every opportunity. Which made me think of Luke, naturally. Wondering what the world and more specifically UK plc will hold for him as a future maths graduate? And I made a mental note to suggest he should learn Mandarin!

After that, I suppose in a bid to lighten up the gloom, I hit on the subject of women. Yes, women in all their fascinating mystery and variety. If I live to be a hundred, I will never understand them! And being in pragmatic mode, I concluded that on the whole, this past couple of years, for all the dullness of cooking for one and the emptiness of the bed, I have been better off. Reaping the modest rewards of the single life: the peace, the freedom, the self-indulgence – as opposed to the pointless stalemate with Moira.

But then the plain truth struck me: of all the women with whom I have rubbed shoulders (professionally speaking) – the female physicians and surgeons, the radiographers, the young nurses, the sisters – of all those, only one would interest me. Leila. Dusky, warm-hearted, unobtainable Leila. Of course, not for the first time, I was telling myself, had circumstances been different, I'd have been tempted to make a move long ago – and deluding myself that she might not have resisted because I know she, too, has sensed the spark of attraction between us. Perhaps, like me, she has thought that, as fellow clinicians, we could understand the pressures and frustrations of our profession in a way our respective spouses have never been able, or willing, to.

Such self-delusion about voluptuous middle-eastern, married paediatricians is unhealthy and so, in the small hours – what else? My thoughts turned back to Violette. Call me Madame, she said. Madame! Glorious title, that, with all it implies; respectability, maturity and, usually, matrimony. I remember starting on the inside of the orifice, slowly working around the circle with the file wrapped in the abrasive paper, rubbing away at the tiny ridges and irregularities of the wood. Was she wearing a wedding ring? I should have noticed when she took her glass of water. No, I don't think there was a ring. But given her unwillingness to shed light on her marital status ('C'est moi qui pose les questions') it seemed quite legitimate to speculate. So, grabbing a well-deserved rest from sanding and buffing, I finished off the Stella and entertained myself with my scenarios, in French, naturally.

Scénario 1: Mariée avec un monsieur anglais. Barry, par exemple. Expert de Marketing. Habite une maison agréable à Wimbledon Village. Possiblement des enfants.

Scénario 2: Mariée avec Monsieur Lorance. Madame habite Wimbledon, Monsieur (bureaucrat) habite Paris ou Bruxelles. Eurostar pour les weekends ensemble. Question: Possibilité, dans l'absence de Monsieur, pour Madame Violette de 'flirter' avec les clients… ?

Scénario 3: Divorcée. Habite un appartement à Wimbledon en solo.

Scénario 4: Divorcée, cohabitant avec le boyfriend anglais. Steve, probablement.

Scénario 5: Non mariée. Habite un appartement avec le poodle.

Scénario 6: Non mariée. Cohabite avec une collègue ou partenaire féminine.

Ah, yes, that was a bit of harmless speculation, thinking up assorted situations of varying probability and absurdity. Not to mention complexity. Because with Violette, there just had to be complexity – layer upon layer of it! And what on earth would I want with a complicated female – *une femme avec bagages*? When quite obviously, I should be looking for a relaxed, straightforward, secure type; ie someone who could make my life a little smoother, rather than complicate it further!

I must have started applying the beeswax then, treating my tired eyes to the sight of the grain markings of the ash rippling out beautifully. Then at the unseemly hour of quarter past three, I found myself concluding that complexity is not necessarily a bad thing. As with wine, obviously. After all, where would be the pleasure in wine without complexity, without the bouquet and the subtle development on the palate? The flint and green apples of a Pouilly fumé; the spiced blackberry and velvety finish of a Gevrey Chambertin... Or on a more humble level, take the example of the memorable Swiss white the hotelier served us the other year in the Rhône Valley. The Fendant – an unknown quantity with an intriguing name. Strangely irresistible.

Yes, what an astonishing little wine that was – product of the high, sunny slopes of the Valais. When it arrived, after the anticipation, I remember slight disappointment at the bottle – plain, clear glass, nothing fancy, with a simple label. And such an unexpectedly pale colour, like one of those sunstarved English wines, rather than one from warm Continental climes. Ah but the revelation when the cork was pulled; the complex, aromatic bouquet and the dry, gravelly first taste, followed by the *pétillance*, tingling quite deliciously on the tongue. Yes, a surprisingly unpredictable, capricious little wine, balancing acidity with sweetness, and finishing with that memorable hint of delicious, sun-ripened fruit...

CHAPTER 4

She was late. Annoyingly late. So there I was at ten past seven, decidedly edgy, glancing out of the dining room window for the first sign of the Volvo. In a bid to keep my cool, I was indulging in imaginary reprimands: Madame la Maîtresse, la classe commence à sept heures – oui, sept heures du soir. Vous n'arrivez pas et je vous paie pour le privilège! C'est sérieux.

Naturally, doubts started to creep in: was it merely a case of lateness or a total no-show? In fact, was I already blacklisted for my audacity in challenging Madame over the correct pronunciation of *intime*?

The phone rang at seven fifteen or so. 'Allo, c'est Violette...' Pitiful tale of the leaking washing machine and the emergency plumber! Did I believe her? Fifty-fifty. In retrospect, I suppose it was a sign of things to come; a taster of her unpredictability, her sense of the dramatic. But at least the delay gave me time to check the dozen sentences on tenses she had handed me as homework at the end of our first session. Some were straightforward, but others, seemingly easy, were deceptive.

She met him at the Louvre.

I pondered that one for quite a while before coming up with my clever little dodge.

Elle a rencontré le monsieur au Louvre.

(Yes, I thought that was neat, dispensing with the grammatical complexities of the *him* and opting for the much simpler *monsieur!*)

It was while I was ploughing through the little red book of French verbs, checking out the compound tenses, that the bell rang and there she was in the low rays of the sun. All sweetness and light, apologising for the delay.

Striking difference in style this time, I noticed. Out with the schoolmistressy linen suit and in with the younger slinky look. Yes, for her second appearance she chose the long, dark skirt with the buttons down one side – many of the lower ones undone (for ease of movement, possibly, or mere effect?). I recall she also wore a greenish-gold v-neck top and a pendant. As for her hair, it was less severe this time – half-up, half-down, whatever they call that.

As well as the executive case, she was carrying a neat CD player and in the dining room we found a suitable place for it, on the table by the window on her side. Once it was plugged in and operational, I offered her a drink.

'Madame, vous désirez le Perrier? Ou possiblement le vin – Shiraz, Chardonnay... Gewurztraminer d'Alsace?'

Her face lit up.

'Oh, le Gewurztraminer – j'adore! Mais juste un petit verre – a little glass.'

When I brought through our wine (gold medal, Concours des Grands Vins d'Alsace) she had donned the little spectacles, and was poring over my homework sheet, attached to her clipboard. She looked up and gave me a pleasant smile.

'Your first two sentences are perfect. Bravo!'

'Merci.'

Then, of course, she spotted my attempt to sidestep the issue in the sentence about the Louvre.

'Ah, Michel, vous avez triché! You cheated!'

'Oh I wouldn't say that.' We exchanged slightly challenging glances. 'I thought I'd come up with a pretty neat solution, actually. I mean, whether we say 'she met *him*' or 'she met *the man*', the net effect is the same: ie a *male* met a *female* in the Louvre!'

She pursed her lips in a French pout. 'Hmm… well, yes, I understand your point of view, Michel, and the sentence you wrote is correct but I devised the question deliberately to test your knowledge of French pronouns – those little words for him and her and it and so on. You English, you hate them, don't you?'

Teasing glance across the table.

'Well, I admit they're hardly riveting.'

'Bon,' She produced one of those fantastic French shrugs. 'I give you the mark anyway for your *ingéniosité*.'

'Merci, Madame.' I gave her a grateful smile and relished my little victory.

Then came the treacherous tar pits; reflexive verbs in the perfect tense, the passive, the dreaded subjunctive. Naturally, I didn't excel there. Being the true professional, she explained how I'd made a hash of them and wrote out the correct sentences for me in her neat, loopy handwriting. I think she awarded me eight out of twelve.

We raised our glasses.

'Santé Madame!'

'Santé!'

She didn't drink straightaway, pausing to inhale.

'Mm, ce bouquet parfumé… Les roses, les raisins, c'est délicieux…'

A discerning palate, evidently. We both sipped our wine for a few moments, and then she began delving into her briefcase –

for her mobile, I imagined. No sign thus far. But no; looking slightly ill at ease, she produced the pair of slim A4 documents and set them on the table. And when she spoke, tension had crept into her voice.

'So – now we must engage in a little formality: the contract.'

'Contract?'

'Yes. You see, we didn't have time to do it last week.'

'Ah…'

'But don't look so concerned, Michel. It is just a formality, as I said, so that we know what to expect of each other.'

Was it some kind of joke? I remember sitting there in a daze, wondering what the hell was going on, as she came over and handed me my copy for perusal. Eight clauses, for pity's sake, all immaculately typed in French legalese!

Accord

Il est convenu entre la professeur, Violette Lorance, et l'étudiant, Doctor Michael Westover, que…

It is agreed between the tutor and the student that… At first sight, it all seemed pretty standard: terms of payment, cancellation notice, provision of a clean, adequate study room. Yes, perfectly reasonable. But then some more unusual stipulations appeared. Notably Clauses 4 and 5:

Article 4

Les deux parties se comporteront d'une manière professionnelle dans un cadre de respect mutuel.

She produced a strained smile. 'So, I am sure you understand it, Michel: both parties will behave in a professional, respectful manner.'

'Sure. I understand perfectly.'

'Good.'

'Although it begs the question: what sort of client would *not* behave appropriately or respectfully?'

Her eyebrows shot up. 'Oh, you would be surprised! One or two of the men of course… Sometimes they try to, how we say in French: *profiter de l'occasion*.'

'*Profiter de l'occasion!* How extraordinary, I thought that had all died out.'

'Oh no. They still exist, believe me. *Les frustrés, les misogynes*.' She reached for her little glass and took a sip. 'Yes, professional women have to be very careful, you know.'

'Evidently… Well, moving on swiftly, how about Article 5? Am I correct in interpreting it as: *The student will avoid all physical contact with the tutor…?*'

'Yes. Correct.'

'Bit one-sided, isn't it?'

'How do you mean?' Slight creasing of her brow.

'Well, I note the clause doesn't consider the other way round.'

'Ha! Docteur Westover – do you imagine there is a danger I will beat you up?'

She had a point, being all of eight stone odd.

'Of course not; I was merely pointing out an interesting discrepancy.'

'Maybe you should have been a lawyer.'

'Maybe. But somehow I found anatomy more appealing than the letter of the law.'

Clause 6 was positively tame by comparison, concerning compulsory homework and the copyright of her teaching materials. But then came number seven, the snake in the grass.

Again I asked her for clarification. She adjusted her spectacles and read out the wording like a newsreader. I got the gist.

'Article 7: L'étudiant respectera l'autorité de la professeur… et acceptera tout jugement… et toute mesure de correction qui semblera nécessaire à la professeur.'

She looked up and smiled nicely. 'So, translate please, Michel.'

'The student shall respect the authority of the tutor in all matters and – let me get this clear – will accept all her judgements and *all corrective measures* as deemed necessary by the tutor. Is that so?'

'Yes.' She gave me one of her long, schoolmistressy looks. 'But of course, the situation of disrespecting the tutor will not arise in future, will it?'

'Heavens no!'

The final clause was the typical catch-all: any breach of the terms will result in the termination of the contract and the immediate cessation of tuition.

'So, Docteur Westover,' – pleasant, expectant smile – 'are you willing to accept the terms of the agreement?'

We duly signed and dated, then exchanged copies, which provided my first sight of Madame's signature – classically French, with extravagant loops and flourishes on the capitals.

After the signing ceremony, she carefully replaced the lid on her iridescent fountain pen before stowing her copy of the contract in her case and proceeding to adopt a brisk tone:

'So, let's move on.'

Except I hadn't quite filed away that one nagging question: what sort of twisted mind produces a contract like that? The mind of a control freak? Or some embittered man-hater? Quite possibly. Or, then again, could it be the mentality of a victim? Someone stung once too often by life's nasty surprises; someone determined to have it all sewn up for next time. Is that how you were, Violette?

After the contract, listening to the weather forecast was light relief. With a casual 'Alors, Michel, la méteo' she reached over to press the play button then sat back, no doubt wondering how I would handle the cheery monsieur's predictions:

Prévision pour samedi, 21 juillet: du soleil partout!

She paused the tape.

'So, what is the weather?'

'Sunny everywhere.'

'Good. Now listen for the temperatures.'

Then Monsieur Méteo picked up speed:

Vingt-cinq degrés à Rennes et Roscoff, vingt-six à Lille. A Paris et Nancy … ving-huit ou vingt-neuf degrés…

Another pause, an expectant look.

'Twenty-five in Rennes, twenty-six in Lille, high twenties in Paris and Nancy.'

'Good. Now listen to the end.'

Dans le sud, vous aurez de belles températures: trente degrés à Bordeaux et Biarritz, trente-et-un à Montpellier et Nîmes. Pour Cannes, Nice et Ajaccio trente-deux ou trente-trois degrés. Ce n'est pas fini, Caligula!

Simplicity itself – scorchio on the Côte d'Azur! But as for the last word…

'What was that bit about Caligula?'

'Caligula? Are you sure?' She was frowning, clearly puzzled.

'Yes, definitely, right at the end. Something like: c'est pas fini Caligula.'

'Ah, *la canicule!* Ce n'est pas fini, *la canicule* – the heatwave is not finished … Ha-ha, Caligula! That's funny.'

And she had a little laugh to herself while I was inwardly deriding her native language! Still, at least she had lightened up, after the intensity of the contract. So it seemed a good moment for a break.

'Madame, vous désirez un chocolat?'

A mystified look while I went to fetch the tin but on my return her expression had changed to one of delight:

'Oh, Maxim's de Paris!'

She took one square, unwrapped it and then, consciously or subconsciously (will I ever know?) treated me to the spectacle: la Maîtresse, sitting back from the table, nibbling at her *carré de chocolat,* one leg crossed high over the other, showing off a nicely sculpted knee and an inviting expanse of much of her left thigh. A detail that apparently had escaped her attention.

'Mmm, c'est bon, ce chocolat noir.'

And then I was treated to the fascinating ritual of her kissing her fingertips, one by one.

'Mmm... Merci, Michel. Mm, c'était exquis.'

With that she straightened up in the chair, adjusted her skirt with wonderful nonchalance, and looked across engagingly.

'So, to finish, we will talk a little bit about your 'olidays in France. Alors Michel, quelle est votre région préférée?'

'La côte d'Azur.'

'Pourquoi?'

'Pour le climat très agréable. Et les villes – Nice, Menton, Antibes… Les restaurants, les fruits de mer, et la Mediterranée bleue, naturellement.'

Then she had me describing the time we came down with the boat – the *'yote'* as she endearingly called it. But I had to set her straight about the scale of it; even showed her a photo of *Entre Deux Mers* to dispel her visions of us leading a Riviera lifestyle on a luxury yacht.

'C'était un Trailer-Sailor, Madame – très modeste. Mais idéal pour Luke et moi, pour les petites aventures.'

'Alors Michel, racontez-moi de vos aventures dans le *yote* de plaisance.'

So we talked about our little trips out on the boat, about snorkelling and rock-pooling and young Luke's acute embarrassment at the sight of topless girls. (Les filles en demi-bikini, I said. Topless, she said!) Then our attempts at fishing; the memorable time when skinny-armed Luke, all of thirteen, reeled in that monstrous-looking spiny scorpionfish lurking among the seaweed.

'Et votre femme, Moira?'

'Ah, elle préfère visiter les musées, les boutiques, les salons de beauté…'

I could feel myself getting into deep waters, explaining that Moira had never much liked the boat, especially after the unfortunate accident during tacking, when she got hit with the boom.

'Oh, your poor wife!'

'Yes, Luke was a little over-zealous that time. Luckily it wasn't serious. Anyway, after that we agreed – quite amicably – to do our own things. So she would luxuriate with a book by the pool or take herself off to Nice, to trundle around the antiques shops, while Luke and I would go for a sail or a drive on the Corniches. or inspect the bizarre creatures at the fish markets – flying gurnard, octopus, sea urchin, even conger eels.'

All the while, as we were talking, sometimes in English but more often in French, my confidence grew and the language seemed to flow more and more smoothly. Yes, that is quite a skill you have, Violette, coaxing reminiscences and anecdotes from your students, so casually yet persuasively: *Racontez-moi ça, Michel... Oh, que c'est fascinant...* And I'll admit, there's a certain buzz – a kind of glamour, I suppose – of engaging in French conversation with an attractive Gallic tutor. In fact, I was starting to feel confident – until I was virtually accused of neglecting my wife.

'Mais Moira, elle se sentait isolée, abandonnée un petit peu?'

'Abandonnée? Non, pas du tout.'

So I began to explain the pragmatic basis for the arrangement: plenty of sailing and physical activity for an adolescent lad and his dad, and culture and retail therapy for his mother and her friends who popped down to the Riviera for the weekend. And I emphasised our family excursions: the Gorges du Verdon, Grasse, the hillside village of la Turbie. Not forgetting the classic attempt to interest Moira in the amazing clifftop garden with the ruined castle at Eze. I even fished out a few photos showing the views over the coast and Cap Ferrat.

'It looks very nice, Eze. Did your wife like it?'

'No, not especially; terracotta roofs and architectural cacti aren't her scene, nor the steps and the cobbled streets which played merry hell with her shoes. And it was a very hot day, I remember.'

'What a pity. So what did she do?'

'Stuck it for a bit and then drove to Monaco.'

'Oh.' She was looking thoughtful, adjusting her pendant, which had strayed slightly off centre. I sensed what was coming. 'You know, Michel, it seems a bit strange, these 'olidays – travelling all this way to the south of France with the boat, and

56

then you and your son, you do one thing, and your wife, she does something else.'

'Well, OK, I admit it isn't the classic family holiday but at the time we all seemed happy enough.'

'Seemed? You said: we all *seemed* happy. But underneath, below the surface, what was happening?'

Suddenly it was uncannily like a session with the late Professor Anthony Clare!

'Well, with hindsight, you could say our separate activities were symptomatic of the underlying problem.'

'Symptomatic? This is the doctor's word! But what does this mean?' She was looking at me intently across the table.

'Well, it means basically, over the years, Moira and I both changed – went off in opposite directions. Different tastes, different ambitions, different friends... became two different people, basically.'

'Tell me about it. Parlez-moi de ça.'

So I found myself telling her, barely noticing if I was speaking English or French, but saying far more than I had intended; good stuff, bad stuff.

'The truth is, we were totally absorbed with our careers. It's a long grind, years and years, working your way up to my level. Exhausting hours, doing nights, weekends etc.'

'And Moira, she was a doctor too?'

'No, she went into accountancy; set up her own agency in London, sank a lot of money into it. So obviously she'd get stressed out about the risk of being squeezed by the competition. Then she'd get at *me* for not being supportive enough or not being around when I was needed with Luke's homework.'

'I see.'

'But to be fair, the pressures aren't the same. Imagine the

awesome responsibility of having a patient's life in your hands. Nothing compares to that. Afterwards, you need a release – go to the gym or just crash out, empty your head. Not a chance of discussing business; you can't even make the simplest decision. Tea or coffee? Sparkling or still? I don't think Moira ever understood that.'

'Elle n'a pas compris.' She smiled gently, looked sympathetic.

'Non, elle n'a pas compris.'

She drained her Gewurztraminer and looked pensive.

'Alors, Michel, en conclusion: avec ces vacances bizarres, les problèmes dans la famille, le stress de votre profession… finalement le mariage s'est désintégré?'

Disintegrated – would I go that far? Think objectively. No sex. No common interests. No conversation, to speak of. Coming home late, drained but ravenous, to some microscopic ready meal plus, if I was lucky, a bit of limp pre-packed salad. The attempts at small talk while Luke was around and then the silences, the ghastly strained silences. Oh yes – and our brilliant façade at dinner parties or medical gatherings, acting the happy couple in front of my colleagues, who were probably doing exactly the same. Then back home to reality. Two strangers under one roof. Poles apart on the sofa; poles apart in the bed.

'C'est exact, Madame. Le mariage a désintégré.'

CHAPTER 5

It is quite something; easily on a par with the Golden Gate or Stonehenge. No, on reflection, better – more mysterious and captivating. And there was something magical about the way it appeared to us – like a mirage, breaking through the morning haze. Barely there and yet unmistakable.

Naturally Luke spotted it first, being the non-driver. Some twenty minutes out of St Malo, I suppose, not long after joining the Route de la Baie. I was too distracted by the sudden crop of oyster farms appearing to our left to see, rising up beyond the lines of wooden stakes and nets in the vast grey bay, the distant silhouette, like a surreal floating fortress.

She must have seen the Mont-Saint-Michel hundreds of times – in brilliant sunshine, sheeting rain, hail and thunderstorms, at high tide and low tide… even emerging from a blanket of fog. Also she would have seen it on many an overcast day like ours when the sky looms heavy over the land. Neither Luke nor I had envisaged such an eerily flat, almost bleak landscape with that long, raised dyke and mudflats bordering the bay. Incredible to think that this place – more like a slice of Holland – is just as much a part of France as the scintillating Riviera.

So, this was Violette's patch of Normandy: miles of sage-green salt meadows and grazing sheep, little field strips, bounded by lines of poplars; a big sky and the vast expanse of wet sand merging into murky sea. And yes, without doubt there is a certain sleepy charm about the scenery – but nothing dramatic. Which is why, I suppose, they built that extravagant pile of granite sitting a little way offshore and suddenly taking you by surprise. Both Luke and I noticed the way it seemed to loom larger and clearer by the minute until, within the final mile or so, there it was: crisp, sharp-edged ramparts and buttresses, rooflines, windows, pinnacles and the soaring spire.

It was as we were parking among the hundreds of cars and I was cursing our stupidity for coming in August, that Madame's words came back to me: *'C'est magnifique en silhouette.'* And true, the Mont-Saint-Michel is definitely far more beautiful, more mysterious, as a distant, hazy mirage than in all its imposing grandeur close up with the tourists gaping at it.

Still, we did what we came to do: joined the throng entering through the splendid gateway and wandering the steep cobbled street; ventured onto the ramparts and the lookout towers; explored little nooks and alleyways off the main street. It was a long, drawn-out haul up all the steps to the abbey, past the sprawling fig tree growing out of a crevice, then onward and upward, ever conscious of those massive walls rising out of the rockface.

After that, alas, the usual anti-climax of queues, ticket desks, bureaucracy and then shuffling *en masse* through narrow corridors and chapels. But it was all worth it – to see the crypt, the splendid, light refectory, and the cloisters on the top level, a medieval roof garden, no less, with that sheer drop down to the sea just the other side. But, best of all, was the west terrace outside the church with the stupendous view over the bay. Standing there, a few hundred feet up, bracing ourselves against the wind coming straight at us over the sludgy tidal flats – that was exhilarating. We definitely earned our *chocolat chaud* and *croque monsieur* after that.

On our way out, Luke insisted on buying me a postcard of my namesake: the golden dragon-slaying archangel, brandishing his sword at the top of the spire: '*L'archange Saint Michel triomphant du dragon.*'

Afterwards we drove back along the bay road and found a suitable spot for an amble over the saltmarshes among the grazing sheep. I should have known it would be all too dull and featureless for Luke, and my pointing out the world heritage status of the Baie du Mont-Saint-Michel cut little ice with him. Well, of course, he would have preferred the buzz of Paris or Marseille to hearing his dad's lame attempts to translate a leaflet on the ecology of saltmarsh. As it happened, our walk was soon curtailed by the ferocious black squall that swept in from the west, instantly turning us into drowned rats and forcing us back to the hotel for a long afternoon of French TV and travel chess.

But the stair rods didn't prevent us from venturing out at seven thirty for dinner in that cosy little restaurant with its '*spécialités normandes*'. We must have looked an odd spectacle, *le papa anglais* and his monosyllabic son, making strained conversation or staring out at the rain. I guess he was bored with my company, missing his girlfriend, and naturally he was fed up with the weather – as he put it so succinctly, it doesn't 'piss down' like that in the south. And the Med is a decent shade of *blue*. I could hear myself sounding like a wise elder, telling him we were unlucky to have that unseasonal depression. But it wouldn't have been any better in Brittany, if we had stayed there. Thank our lucky stars we weren't out at sea in that Force 8.

At least he cheered up when our seafood arrived. Even ceased texting and began picking at the shells with the array of implements. And those *bulots and bigorneaux*... whelks or winkles, whatever, were delicious. He certainly ate his share. Looking at my son across the table, I noticed the change since we'd last met; the fleshier, more masculine jawline, the decent crop of stubble, and longer hair. In fact, suddenly there it was, staring me in the face – uncanny reincarnation of Michael Westover, first year medical student: tall, dark-haired, hazel-eyed youth gangling his way through life.

The lamb – *agneau du pré salé* – was as memorable as the shellfish. Both Luke and I opted for it, our blustery walk among the sheep having whetted our appetite. And unbelievably tender it was, with that distinctive tang of the saltmarsh.

As the meal progressed I remember our conversation began to flow more easily – due in no small part to the excellent local cider and the shot of Calvados in our sorbets. Even when I broached the subject of Rachel, he was surprisingly forthcoming with the details. Psychology student, tall, pretty, long brown hair, great squash player, easy-going – no wonder he was smitten. I suppose we spent a couple of minutes talking about the two of them and the shared house, after which he turned the tables.

'So what about you?'

'What about me?'

'You know…'

'Am I seeing someone, is that what you're asking?'

'Yeah.'

'Not at the moment. I mean, when did I have the time or the opportunity these past couple of years? Moving house, settling the divorce… and let's face it, I'm not passing cute little nurses in the corridor every day now, am I?'

'Be realistic. You should be thinking of the older ones, more your age.'

'Too true. Still, as it happens there aren't many of interest.

Besides, some of the senior ones are quite objectionable – so bolshy, think they know better than us! Then you get the other extreme, the go-getters, trying to sleep their way up the hierarchy! Spot them a mile off...'

'Oh yeah, like the one you used to go on about... what did you call her?'

He stopped piling up the sachets of sugar for a moment, waiting for my reaction.

'You mean Shagpile.'

'Yeah, her.'

'Ah yes... dear old Shagpile Sharon. Don't get many like her, thank god!'

'She was after you!'

'Ah but she didn't get me, Luke. Not a hope... You'd think she'd realise that she's not my league; that I'm more interested in classy, dusky paediatricians, for example.'

'Oh?'

'Yes. With beautiful names, such as Leila.'

'Layla? As in your ancient, warped single?'

'Different spelling from Clapton's. Anyway, I used to see her occasionally in the car park or the corridor. Sometimes we'd have a chat in the canteen... compare notes, exchange gripes... And she'd lend a sympathetic ear about my various trials and tribulations.'

'So you're lusting after Layla, then?'

'Not exactly lusting. Besides, she's married, couple of kids. So strictly off-limits.'

'Very ethical of you.'

'Well, come on, Luke, one failed marriage is enough. I'm not in the business of wrecking other people's. Agreed, some of my colleagues have a more liberal take on that but there we are...'

'Ah, shame... poor old Dad, no one on the horizon.'

'Thanks for the sympathy. Very touching.'

'Hey what about what's her name... the French one?'

'Violette!'

'Whatever. Do you like her?'

'She's quite nice.'

'Think she likes you?'

'No idea!'

'Oh come on, you can suss out her type... I mean is she the typical French woman type... I mean, does she flirt with you?' That impish grin of his, his cheeks reddened by the cider.

Good question. What do you call that, when your personal tutor sits a few feet away from you, oh so nonchalantly revealing a serious slice of thigh? Is that flirting or just a cynical power game to tantalise the student? Whatever you call it, she's a master at it.

'Well, it's hard to say. She's unpredictable, bit of a deep one. Complicated, you know, neurotic...'

'Not your type?'

'No, not really...'

Our memorable desserts arrived: my enormous slice of *tarte normande*, all buttery pastry and succulent apple, and Luke's equally magnificent *crêpe au chocolat*. After that, all we could do was sit in silence, stuffed to the gunnels, in the cosy glow of over-indulgence. The rain was still lashing the windows and outside the lights were streaks and blurs. And a mile or so down the road, the Mont-Saint-Michel was surviving another battering.

While we were waiting for Madame la patronne to come and clear away, we began perusing the map of the local area, reviewing the possibilities. Our deliberations obviously intrigued the elderly, bespectacled monsieur at the bar, who kept looking over our way. Eventually he couldn't resist coming over to offer his assistance.

'Je peux vous aider?'

'Ah, oui Monsieur. Nous désirons visiter la région. Vous pouvez recommander...'

'Ah, oui. Alors vous avez beaucoup de possibilités...' Leaning over the table, his leathery hand resting on the map, he delivered his run-down on unmissable attractions: Bayeux tapestry, Rouen, the cider farms and distilleries, the landing beaches... and, much closer to home, there was always Avranches, which he indicated with his fingernail, a mere 18 kilometres away.

'C'est intéressant, Avranches?'

'Oui Monsieur, Avranches, c'est une ville historique. Là, par exemple, vous avez un musée moderne avec les manuscrits médievals du Mont-Saint-Michel. Et le jardin botanique avec vue panoramique...'

After that it was only polite to introduce ourselves and Albert seemed pleased to join us for a chat. He was retired he said ('retraité... et marié depuis 40 ans!') Then we talked about hailing from London and Luke being 'étudiant de mathématique', and we filled him in on our crowded tour of the Mont-Saint-Michel. Albert rambled on about the pressure of tourists and new measures to prevent the bay silting up. Yes, he was pretty well informed about his part of France. Moreover, as well as acting as unpaid tourist guide, he did a great job of initiating us into one of Normandy's legendary social rituals: *le Café-Calva*. It was his idea to go to the bar to order it from Madame and when she brought the tray with the fresh coffee and our shots of Calvados, he became quite animated.

'Alors, regardez!' Concentrating as he picked up the cafétière: 'Un petit peu de café...'

Luke was as fascinated as I was by his ceremony: sloosh of hot coffee into a cup, then drink all but the dregs.

'Et maintenant le Calva...'

In went the good stuff into the coffee residue, then with a practised hand he began swirling it around the cup, then offering it to my nose:

'Sentez!'

Fantastic aroma.

'Et maintenant, goutez! Goutez, Monsieur!'

Rich, warm Calvados, infused with the tang of good, strong coffee. And the kick afterwards.

'Ah, c'est très bon, ça! Try it Luke.'

'C'est bon?' Albert smiled.' Ça s'appelle la rincette.'

La rincette – neat little name that. After that we did several repeat performances. The next one Albert called *la surincette*. Then came the *coup de grâce*. The fourth, I think, he called *serpent dans les fleurs*. All the while, between sips of Calvados, we were chatting, mainly in French with a bit of franglais thrown in and Albert wove his entertaining yarn. The three days of freedom he was enjoying while his good wife was visiting her sister in Coutances. The relaxed smile on his face said it all.

'Ah, c'est magnifique! Trois jours de liberté...' I got the general drift: he was relishing the leisurely breakfast, the constitutional with the dog down by the Bay of Mont-Saint-Michel, then back home to fit in a little repainting of the woodwork before joining his friends in the café for lunch and a sociable afternoon. Not that he was idle, talking about his constant battle against the elements. Afterwards, I recall Luke calling me a pseud for saying 'Oui, oui, absolument. Terrible!' when I could hardly claim the same struggle with gales and salt air in Putney!

After Albert left us, pumping our hands vigorously like an old friend, and wishing us *bonnes vacances*, we spent ages, waiting for the bill. Not that it mattered in our cosy, alcohol-induced inertia. I remember we began comparing the drinking habits of the French and the English and suddenly I found my son quizzing me on my alcohol consumption; totting up my units on the proverbial paper serviette and declaring sanctimoniously that I was one of these middle-class boozers who drink far too much and, as a representative of the medical profession, a total hypocrite!

After that we settled up and headed out into the deluge for a sobering battering by the elements and the dash back to the hotel. And duly dried out, still warm from the meal and the *Café-Calva*, we both slept like logs.

Avranches. Cité des manuscrits. Cité de Violette! A lofty, cultured place, set up on that hill above the coastal plain of la Baie. And, to our joy after the previous day's deluge, a 'Cité' bathed in sunshine. We parked up in the large main square on the plateau, near to the twin-towered church, and conveniently close to the Jardin des Plantes – distinctly French with its imposing wrought iron gates and extravagant bedding displays. Not forgetting that brilliant sculpture of the female form rising out of a massive chunk of sequoia.

It seemed that all the good workers of the town were in the *jardin* for their lunch break, strolling through singly or in pairs to the sound of classical music piped from cleverly concealed speakers. I remember commenting to Luke that it was like a small French version of Regent's Park, only better, with that magnificent view. We had to go to the far end of the gardens to find it, passing under the shade of the horse chestnut trees and emerging onto the terrace with the balustrade and the telescopes. And across the plain, at the far end of the winding river, there it was – the distant *monument* in the expanse of gleaming sea; a tiny dark triangle, easily overlooked or mistaken for a large rock.

As for the other landmark, Luke spotted that later on: the Sherman tank, sitting on a large roundabout at one end of the town. *Thunderbolt*, no less! Close by, as I recall, was the statue of General Patton, Libérateur d'Avranches. To think, Luke assumed I would know all the details of the liberation! I really wonder sometimes just how old he thinks I am.

We had plenty of time for a drink under the trees near to the *hôtel de ville* and as we sat, relaxing, there were all those signs encouraging us to see the medieval manuscripts of Mont-Saint-Michel. But somehow both of us were too lethargic to do justice to those historic, illuminated scrolls. So we sat and watched the world go by and, yes, remembering what Violette had said about going home to Normandy for her holidays, I was keeping half an eye open for a dark Volvo with the local 50 registration plate. Of course, there were plenty of Renaults, Peugeots and Citroens, the odd little Ford – cinquante, cinquante, cinquante – but no black Volvo saloons.

But naturally it crossed my mind that there was a possibility of coming across her on foot, as we explored the quieter streets around the castle. Crazily, I had some hazy approximation of her floating around in my head: a very French Violette in a summer outfit, suddenly coming up the steep narrow street towards us with a look of astonishment. Or just emerging from an *épicerie* with a basket containing a Camembert and a lettuce… Ludicrously stereotyped image, really.

I remember, that afternoon there were two possible sightings: both late thirties, slim build, shoulder length brown hair. One with specs, one without. But not Violette; no, definitely not her. Wrong shoes. Wrong posture. Wrong jizz as twitchers would say.

And of course she wasn't down at the bay, early evening, when we drove to Pointe du Grouin Sud to take some photos of the Mont-Saint-Michel at sunset. Nice little drive, that, following the river downstream, passing country gardens with their heavy crops of apples, pears, even peaches. At the estuary, with its curiously jagged, reef-like rocks, Luke persuaded me to scramble down the bank to the shore. After being cheek-by-jowl with the coach-loads of tourists at le Mont, at last we had the luxury of the view across the water all to ourselves.

There was barely a breath of wind as we waited for the sunset to reach its peak; watching small channels oozing in the wet sand and wading birds scurrying around. We messed about, Luke skimming stones, me scavenging for driftwood, while the sky turned golden behind the grey silhouette with the wispy spire; far more substantial now, seen from the shore, than the insignificant cone viewed from the Avranches hilltop.

On our way back to the car Luke almost walked into the spider's web strung from the thorn bush; freaked out at the curious-looking occupant with its waspish colours and its legs in pairs – quite unlike our own spiders. Another example of the different species to be found just across the Channel!

So, mission accomplished, back we drove to the hotel on the plateau for our lobster dinner. Afterwards, we had a stroll in the illuminated Jardin des Plantes and we persuaded ourselves we could see faint lights on the monument. Then we headed back to plan our onward journey to Granville and up the coast of the Cherbourg Peninsula, or le Cotentin.

We both needed our early night, hitting the sack at ten thirty. It crossed my mind that Violette might be doing the same thing, snug in her nightie or pyjamas. A mere stone's throw perhaps from our hotel – closer even than Wimbledon Village is to Putney Heath.

CHAPTER 6

The Normandy jaunt seemed a distant memory by the time we met for the third lesson. Already mid September and I had to put on the outside light for her. When she arrived at the agreed time of seven thirty I remember being struck by two things. First, her punctuality. And second, her sea-green suit and the luxurious silk scarf with hummingbirds. With her hair up in a high ponytail and more noticeable make-up this time, there was something of the air hostess about her.

'Bonsoir Madame. Comment allez-vous?'

'Très bien, merci.' Breezy, confident smile. 'Et vous?'

'Très bien.'

Once installed at the table, she immediately began delving into her handbag, not, as I imagined, for her mobile or fountain pen, but for a sachet of peppermint tea. And having duly supplied her with a cup of hot water, to facilitate the ceremonial dunking of the bag on a string, I sat down opposite and we began.

'Well, it's been seven weeks, so I hope you're not expecting me to produce scintillating French tonight.'

I caught a glint of her eyes as she glanced across.

'Come on, Michel. Where is your spirit, your *dynamisme*? Let's start with a simple question. What you did today... Alors, qu'est-ce que vous avez fait?'

'Moi, j'ai visité un restaurant italien à midi avec un collègue. Et nous avons discuté l'utilisation de *Botulinum* toxin dans l'urologie. Le Botox!'

'Le Botox? Dans l'urologie?'

'Oui, c'est un traitement moderne et révolutionnaire...' Then it seemed fitting to elaborate on the technique of injecting it into the bladder wall and the beneficial effects on patients with urge incontinence. 'C'est fascinant...'

'Ah oui. Fascinant, mais un peu bizarre...' She frowned and then – no doubt to pay me back for going into unnecessary urological detail – she gabbled something about *séduction* and *gastronomie de Toscane*, then she was looking at my blank face expectantly.

'You didn't understand the question, Michel? I was asking you if your Italian lunch was good. I ask it more simply: Le repas italien, c'était bon?'

'Ah oui, délicieux, Madame...' I gave her a weak smile and did my best to convert anchovy-stuffed peppers and Spaghetti Carbonara into passable French.

'Hm, Spaghettis à la Carbonara c'est très riche, ça... c'est mauvais pour la digestion.' She had that classic disapproving tone of the health-conscious French who obsess about salt and saturated fats. 'Une infusion, par contre, c'est bon.' Sipping her minty-smelling brew, telling me I should try herbal infusions. 'Ac-tu-al-ly in France it is normal to take *infusion* for the good digestion. We don't drink so much coffee or tea as you English.'

'I guess you don't.'

'So, Michel,' – a pleasant smile – 'tell me about your holidays. Vous avez visité la Côte d'Azur?'

'Non, Madame. Luke et moi, nous avons visité la Bretagne... Et la Normandie aussi.'

'Normandie?' Raised eyebrow. 'Où – Deauville, Honfleur, Rouen? Les plages du débarquement – the landing beaches?'

'C'est compliqué... J'explique.'

So that was my cue to describe our crossing over to St Malo and the couple of nights in Dinard, followed by the leisurely drive into Normandy and our stopovers along the Cherbourg Peninsula – Granville, Barneville-Carteret, then over to the landing beaches and up to the port of Saint Vaast-la-Hougue. Finally, keeping the best until last, I took great pleasure in casually mentioning that we had managed to stop off at the Mont-Saint-Michel. Of course, those magic words brought out her radiant smile.

'Enfin! Vous avez visité le Mont!'

'Oui, c'est magnifique.'

'Ah oui, magnifique. Répétez: man-yif-eeque!'

'Man-yif-eeque!'

After that we had a look at my photos. My artistic efforts went down well, especially the atmospheric ones of le Mont in the golden sunset, and Luke silhouetted on the rocks by the river mouth. She soon recognised the spot, looking at me with suspicion.

'But this is Pointe du Grouin Sud, yes? Just a little distance from Avranches!'

'Yes, we called in there, too, actually.'

'You went to Avranches?' Reproachful look. 'But you didn't tell me!'

'Well it was spontaneous, a spur of the moment thing. How do you say that in French?'

'Un caprice.'

'Exactly. C'était un caprice, Madame.'

She began leafing through the photos of the botanic garden and came across the abysmal one of me posing by the balustrade with the distant speck of Mont-Saint-Michel, looking like a printing blemish.

'Who took your picture – your son?'

'Yes. I've seen better ones.'

'So you don't like photos of yourself?' Wide, enquiring eyes looking into mine.

'Not particularly. Well, who does? Seeing the pounds go on, the receding hairline.'

'Receding?'

'It means balding, well, sort of… You know, pretty much the same lousy effect!'

'Oh but Michel…' Lips pursed in thought. 'You shouldn't be so negative! You see, to describe your hair, I would prefer to say…' (The nerve of it, looking at my hairline as if assessing a second-hand Chesterfield for wear and tear!) 'Yes, I would say: *dégarni. Un peu dégarni.*'

Dégarni! Thanks for that one, Violette, dear. Ungarnished! Still, infinitely more stylish than bald or receding.

After that, she threw in the informal test on Mont-Saint-Michel and the area. What notable facts could I tell her? Not surprisingly, the incredible tides sprang to mind, one of the greatest ranges in the world, and fast and furious, racing in like a galloping horse, as I'd read in a brochure. Then I managed to dredge up something about the pilgrims of the past, risking the perils of tide and quicksand to reach their destination.

'Oui, oui. C'est exact.' Nodding vigorously. 'Et la date de la construction du Mont-Saint-Michel? Et la légende?'

Looking at me expectantly, waiting for the magic words to drop from my lips. I shook my head.

'Désolé, Madame… I'm afraid somehow we missed those crucial bits of information. But then it was the height of the tourist season. Cheek by jowl – impossible to linger.'

'Oh yes, it is crowded in August during the day. Much better to go for the *visite nocturne* with illumination. Or, even better, you stay in a hotel on le Mont. Then you experience the *ambiance* of the citadel in the sea, and you feel the centuries of the history.' Another sip of her medicinal brew. 'Now, shall I tell you the historic date for the Mont-Saint-Michel – when the first stone was laid?'

'Please.'

'OK...' Dramatic pause. 'En l'an sept cent huit. Vous comprenez?'

'Seven hundred and eight?'

'Exactly. Think of that, thirteen hundred years ago!'

'Amazing.'

'Yes. And since this time people are coming from the corners of the world to experience the mystery, I want to say *la sanctité*... you understand?'

'Sanctity.'

'Yes, exactly. We must respect that sanctity, Michel. Because certainly, we can make great efforts to protect the architecture of le Mont, but also we must preserve the *intimité* of the chapels. We should respect the thousands of people who have come, for the centuries, to offer their prayers and the integrity of their souls.'

She was on a roll, extolling the virtues of her precious monument with that philosophical yet passionate tone I've only ever encountered in French nationals.

'And of course we preserve the legend of Saint Michel. It is beautiful too. Shall I tell you about it?'

'Go ahead.'

'Well, of course, it happened in 708, as you now know, the magical year... So the legend says that Aubert, Bishop of Avranches, suddenly he saw the Archange Michel in an amazing dream, and the archangel commanded him: go and make a building in his honour on that special rock in the sea!'

'Which he did.'

'Yes, he did. And afterwards, over hundreds of years the monks, they were building the wonderful Abbaye and all the marvels we see today. Then finally much later, in the nineteenth century, the figure of the archangel was put right on the top of the … comment dire, *la flèche*.'

'The spire.'

'Yes, the spire. They put a golden Saint Michel on top of the spire.'

'Un instant, Madame.' My interjection startled her as I handed her the postcard of the winged figure with the raised sword, gleaming against blue sky. She was obviously impressed.

'Oh qu'il est magnifique!'

'Oui, Madame. Le Saint Michel…' – somehow the caption on the reverse of the card flashed into my mind – 'triomphant sur le dragon.'

'Oh bravo, Michel!' She looked at me with admiration. 'I think you deserve a little reward for your excellent French. In fact, I have brought something delicious with me from Normandy.'

That wonderful moment: Madame la Professeur delving into her attaché case for the box marked *Confiserie*, then bringing it over to my side of the table.

'Voilà: Les pâtes de fruits.' Varnished pink fingernails holding open the flaps of waxed paper, revealing the tempting array of sweets. She could have been an air hostess in her fitted suit, offering round the barley sugars in preparation for the descent. But no mass-produced barley sugars for the discerning Violette; no, the best handmade fruit jellies – glittering squares of crimson, red, orange…

'Vous désirez? Fraise, cassis, pêche, poire…'

'Fraise. merci!'

Rich jammy sludge of crushed strawberries and sugar –

merveilleux! Before she had selected hers, mine was gone.

'Encore, Michel? Please take another – they are pure fruit and sugar, completely natural.'

The blackcurrant one this time, aromatic and rich, possibly even better than the strawberry. A delicious taste to match the delicious vision of Violette as she returned to her chair, the sea-green suit flattering her curves – and in those few seconds, how was she to know that, as well as relishing the succulent fruit jelly, I was noting her exquisite waist-hip ratio?

'Merci, Madame, pour les bonbons.'

'Je vous en prie.'

'Délicieux – et pas de couleurs artificielles, pas de préservatives.'

Stunned silence and then the eruption of bubbling laughter.

'Oh, *préservatif*, this is a false friend!' And when she controlled herself she enlightened me that I'd just been talking about a lack of condoms.

'So now we must finish our lesson.' She picked up her clipboard and switched back into lecturer mode to deliver her thoughts on the passive. *Le passif*, as she termed it. And we looked at the grammar book and then she offered her own rather curious example, written in felt-tip pen on a sheet of paper: *L'argent a été volé par l'architecte*.

'Translate, Michel.'

'The money was stolen by the architect.'

'Exactly. I think you understand the construction, yes? You see, the mon-ay, *l'argent*, it was passive while it was stolen, *volé*. Now the architect, he did the taking away; we call him the agent and he comes at the end of the sentence. Just like in English. Now, try to make some passives of your own, in English first.'

'OK… The mainsail was wrecked by the storm.'

She raised her eyes.

'Ah yes, of course, you like to think about your *yote*! Well, OK, it's a good example, let's turn it into French. So, Michel, we start with the sail. You know that one?'

'La grande voile…'

'Good. What happened to it?'

'La grande voile a été… ruinée… par la tempête.'

'Bravo! Très bien. Encore un example.'

'Le steak a été grillé par le chef.'

'Good. You really understand the concept. One more?'

'Le patient a été opéré par l'urologue.'

'Perfect. I see there are no problems for you with *le passif*.' She smiled, evidently pleased with my grammar. 'By the way…'

'Yes?'

'Because you just mentioned your work, what kind of patients do you see in *urologie*?'

'All sorts. We see a lot of prostate cancer, benign prostate hyperplasia, bladder cancer, kidney stones, incontinence, erectile dysfunction…'

'Oh…' Slight grimace on her part.

'Yes, all kinds of complex, even debilitating conditions.'

'Hm, yes… and very personal, too.'

'Indeed.'

'But at least you can help your patients with their intimate problems.'

'Absolutely. That's why we're there – to achieve better outcomes, a better quality of life.'

She smiled, sympathetically I thought, then chose to switch to French.

'Bien, Docteur Westover, une question: pourquoi abandonner les opérations? Pourquoi abandonner les pauvres patients pour votre sabbatical?'

Ah. She had me there. And she knew it.

'C'est une situation compliquée, Madame... Très compliquée.' I looked her straight in the eye.

'Bof!' A cool, dismissive shrug and a slightly miffed tone. 'I don't expect for you to tell me because, as you know, we don't discuss our personal *affaires*. After all, we hardly know each other.' She clicked open the catches on her case. 'So, we must finish; we have completed the learning objectives for tonight.'

It was on her way out that the incident occurred; stepping outside, she caught her heel between the metal ruts of the doormat. She pulled up, twisted round and looked perplexed at the sight of her trapped shoe. Naturally I did the gallant bit, stooping down to assist in the liberation.

'Let's hope it hasn't torn the leather.'

I handed over the shoe for inspection.

'Oh, it is just a scratch. Anyway, it is my fault to be wearing heels so narrow like this.'

You said it, Madame!

'They certainly are very high, aren't they? I never cease to marvel at how women walk in perilous FMs like those.'

The word slipped out before I could stop it! Just my luck – with her acute sense of hearing, she noticed.

'FMs? Did you just say FMs?' Her expression: wide-eyed, incredulous, in the glow of the porch light. 'What does it mean?'

'Oh well, hah! No idea, to be honest. That was Moira's expression for high, teetery black shoes.'

'You mean, like mine?'

'Well, yes, pretty much like yours.'

'I see...'

A moment of silence, in which I could tell my comment was being logged for future reference. Yes, with my runaway tongue blurting out those two provocative letters, I'd lost all the good favour gained during our civilised conversation about the Mont-Saint-Michel.

She picked up her case. 'Bon, je m'en vais. Bonsoir.'

As she walked away, the dry click of her heels resounding on the pathway, I tried to redeem myself:

'Hey, what about homework? Would you like to set me some?'

She paused, halfway to her car, jangling her keys, then strolled casually back over.

'Yes, good idea. You can write something for me.'

'What subject?'

'Oh now… Let me think… Ah yes! I know: the perfect thing. You can write a little essay for me on the subject of women's shoes. The title: *Les chaussures pour femmes*.'

'Ah. *Les chaussures pour femmes*… How much do you want, a paragraph?'

'No, about one page please. A4. I am sure you can find something interesting to write.'

'We'll see…'

'But of course you will. In fact, I am expecting it from you… And Michel?'

'Yes?'

'Make sure you explain about the FMs.'

CHAPTER 7

Les chaussures pour femmes... what is there to say on that subject? Apart from the fact that it is quite beyond me why certain women – not to say wives – think nothing of devoting an entire double wardrobe to the things and frittering a fortune on them.

Now if she had given me a *useful* subject to write about: wine for example – where would I begin: les grands crus classés de Bordeaux? Or football – the pleasure one could have from the names alone: Paris Saint-Germain, Olympique de Marseille, Zinedine Zidane... And I would willingly have pondered over the French for back of the net, in off the post, hat trick, joy unconfined... Or she might have asked for my thoughts on the Rugby World Cup, and I could have paid tribute to the stars of the French team. Or even the Tour de France. Yes, sport would have been a dream. Then again, she might have given me a more substantial topic, *La politique de l'Union Européenne*, for example. But women's shoes! Pourquoi, Madame, avez-vous insisté sur ce sujet infernal?

But there it is, she threw down the gauntlet and I am never one to shrink from a challenge. Consequently, for the one and only Violette I put in a good hour of graft with the dictionary on that essay, trying to produce something truly original and thought-provoking. Yes, I was all prepared for her on that rainy Wednesday night in mid October.

One minute past seven, she was at the door. Astonishing

shiny vision: *la Maîtresse en plastique noire*! Zipped up to the neck in her glossy black mac, at least so I presumed.

'Bonsoir Madame... Vous permettez – shall I take your rain-coat?'

'No thanks. Ac-tu-al-ly it's not a coat. It's a dress.'

'Ah...'

Yes, an extraordinary dress in that wet-look fabric – practically down to her ankles with deep side slits. The shoes were high, black and strappy. As for her hair, she wore it swept over to one side and anchored behind her ear. All in all, she was a breathtaking vision of glamour.

We decided on Zinfandel for a change and when I came through from the kitchen, she was looking out of the window with her back to me, showing off her stunning figure in the shiny black wrapping.

'You're very stylish tonight.'

She turned and I caught the little satisfied smile.

'Thank you. It's a unique dress. A friend made it.'

'Nice friend...'

'Yes. Brilliant at *couture*.'

We sat down and began with conversation – the Punch and Judy show in the House of Commons (plus ça change...), the media frenzy surrounding the latest travels of Monsieur le Président. Then we spoke of my recent spin on the London Eye with Edward and Jill in honour of his birthday.

'Edward's my brother. Mon frère. Il est dentiste.'

'Ah, vous êtes une famille médicale, alors. Urologue, dentiste...'

'Oui, exactement.'

Then, to my surprise, she mentioned her father had been a science teacher, and while the going was good I decided to ask her parents' names.

'Mes parents? Ils s'appellent Victor et Arlette… Et mon frère s'appelle Gérard. Et mes nièces adorables, elles s'appellent Alexandra et Nathalie.'

'Yes, I see. And your name, Violette? How did that come about – if I may ask?'

'Well…' a flush of pink came to her cheeks. 'It's simple. My father adores botany and he wanted to name me after a flower. So because I was born in April, my parents decided I would be Violette. It was very unusual at that time; a bit old-fashioned. But today Violette is *à la mode*… Very *in*.'

She smiled and I relished the informality of the moment and that rare insight I'd gleaned into her world.

'So Michel…' (the April violet leaning forward a little in her fetishistic dress!) 'Let's talk about your essay. Did you do it?'

'Of course.'

She took the print-out from my hand, casting her eyes over it for a few seconds, during which she gave nothing away except for the slight raising of an eyebrow, presumably at the last paragraph. Then, briskly and efficiently, my labour of love was cast aside on the table.

'Thank you. We will discuss it a little later. But ac-tu-al-ly I want to do something else with you first.' She began rummaging in her case, surprisingly disorganised for la Maîtresse it seemed to me. 'Yes, here it is… a listening exercise on the subject of the French financial market.'

'La Bourse.' Of course, I was trying to impress her, as she inserted the disc into the machine.

'Oui, la Bourse.'

Ah yes, what an inspired change of plan that was, Violette – inflicting on me that horrendous torrent of financial jargon, percentages and obscure company names. After a deceptively easy start (*Journée frénétique à la Bourse de Paris*) I suffered two minutes of it, fast and furious, as if the guy were commentating on the Derby. I gleaned merely a couple of phrases (*La crise des 'sub-primes'* and *exportations de Chine*) before with considerable relief I saw her reach for the stop button.

'So, Michel, how did you find that – all right?'

'Abysmal. Absolutely abysmal! Hardly got a word.'

'Oh, but Michel, it is a normal financial report from the radio. I suppose the journalist talks quite fast because he is from Paris but I am surprised you found it so difficult.' She leaned across to replay the track. 'But then my students always surprise me – sometimes brilliant, sometimes, how shall I say… a little bit slow, yes?'

'Evidently.'

'OK, listen again for some more phrases, and also there is a complicated date he mentions. I want you to write it for me.'

I suppose I picked up marginally more (*nervosité des investisseurs… Situation qui n'invite pas à l'optimisme…*) but it took three replays to decipher the horrendous date:

milleneufcentquatrevingtdixhuitquatrevingtdixneuf!

'Nineteen ninety-eight/ninety-nine.'

'Enfin! Finalement!' She awarded me an ironic smile. 'So, Michel, we will leave la Bourse, which evidently is not a subject you enjoy, and now you will read me your essay, your *rédaction*.'

My moment of glory! The priceless thoughts of Docteur Michel on the subject of women and their shoes. Now looking back, had I confined my comments to considerations of design and materials and the dictates of fashion, rather than controversial observations on the wearer, no doubt the outcome of the evening would have been entirely different. But no: there it was, like a smouldering firework waiting to go off.

The opening paragraph was harmless enough, with its historical beginning:

'Les femmes et les chaussures, c'est une longue histoire. J'imagine que cela a commencé avec Cléopatra.'

I read it with a certain flair. Then I hit her with some figures: fifteen pairs minimum for the typical woman; six pairs maximum for most men. She motioned with her hand.

'Where did you find the statistique?'

'In my head!'

'Very enterprising. Continue.'

The second paragraph described Moira's shoe collection – forty pairs of every colour and all her matching handbags. An obsession, as I said, which seemed a fair comment to Madame. She didn't object either to my observations on the ultimate price to be paid for wearing pointed shoes:

'Le sacrifice des metatarses et phalanges au nom de la vanité!'

'Metatarses et phalanges! Voilà le docteur qui parle!'

'Oui, Madame!'

Despite her encouragement, I was bracing myself for the next part, which I suspected might ruffle a few feathers. My bold decision to mention male fetishes for thigh-length boots, *bottines* and stilettos. Frowning a little, she leaned forward.

'Continuez!'

So I did, digging myself further and further into *la merde*.

'Pour moi, les 'stilettos' représentent deux sociétés: 1) La société du chic et de la haute couture, et naturellement les stars du cinéma. 2) Le demi-monde de l'érotisme, de la nuit, du trottoir… Les 'filles de joie',

les filles de numéro, qui fréquentent les zones 'rouges' en mini-jupe et FMs (stilettos du genre: Voulez-vous coucher avec moi?)'

She had gone white as a sheet, looking at me with utmost distaste, as if I were a kerb crawler.

'Ah – maybe I should stop there?'

'Oh no! It is fascinating to listen to your ideas. Read the last part.'

'Well if you insist…'

'I do.'

'En conclusion, une question: est-il possible que les chaussures sont les indicateurs sur les femmes… par exemple indicateurs de la personnalité et les préférences de style, indicateurs de la profession, la classe sociale (milieu), et possiblement la prédisposition pour les rencontres amoureuses ou érotiques?'

Madame waited for several seconds to be sure I had finished. Then, in an extraordinary tone I have rarely heard – semi-complimentary, semi sarcastic – she spoke:

'*Félicitations*! In my experience of private tuition, no student has ever produced such a remarkable piece of work. Let me see it again.'

She took it from me and put on her little gold spectacles like an examiner.

'So, you used some good vocabulary. Appropriate use of tenses and you made sure your adjectives agree with the subject… Yes, this was good. But then, for some reason only you can understand, Docteur Westover, you decide to depart from the world of fashion and chic to describe women of a very different kind – *les filles de joie*. What do you mean with this?'

'Well, it's self-evident. I'm sure you know the meaning.'

'But *you* are the writer, you tell me: what is the meaning of *filles de joie?*'

Her eyes… intense and sludgy, like a brooding sea.

'Prostitutes, I mean women selling themselves.'

'Yes, exactly. The stereotypes in mini-skirts and high heels! I must say, I didn't expect this from you, Michel.'

'Well, I was trying to convey the message given by 'FM shoes' – which is what you asked, if you recall. As a matter of fact, I could have been less subtle and spelt out the four letter word in its entire Anglo-Saxon vulgarity.'

'Anglo-Saxon? So you are meaning the f-word? This *perle* of the English language! Oh, I see, I understand now. But the M, what is this for?'

'Me – as in: f*** me.'

I thought I'd restrain myself for her sake. Nonetheless, she raised her eyes.

'But of course. I should have known it.'

She got up from the table and then came the sarcastic teacher bit – walking over to the hallway door, then back to the window and resting against the sill, arms folded tightly below her breast pockets.

'Bien, Docteur Westover. Votre petite 'dissertation' est remarquable. Du point de vue grammatical et stylistique, c'est un succès. Bravo.'

I ventured a modest smile, more of a grimace really.

'Mais du point de vue mentalité, attitude: zéro! Oui – zéro! Et franchement, je suis choquée. Profondément choquée par votre texte, par votre attitude misogyne. Vous comprenez ce terme, misogyne?' Hands on hips now.

'Sure, sexist; misogynous. But I can assure you that was purely unintentional.'

'Hah! This is what you think of me? *Une fille de joie?*' Her eyes were wide, burning into me like lasers. 'A whore!'

'No, that's absurd. I never implied that.'

'But yes, Michel: the other evening you called my shoes FMs and now with your essay, you make very clear what a woman is like who wears shoes like that. So you will certainly think that I look like a woman of the night waiting for *rencontres érotiques*, as you said.'

'No, you've misinterpreted what I said. I was talking about a certain look, a provocative way of dressing associated with women in a certain neighbourhood, difficult social circumstances etc...'

'Who wear the shoes exactly like mine! This is what you mean. High heels, shiny, black – it is obviously to you the symbol of a cheap woman. But ac-tu-al-ly, for your information, my 'FM shoes', to employ your expression, came from a very expensive shop in Bruxelles, Avenue Louise.'

'I don't doubt it.'

'Yes. And in fact, before I meet *you*, Docteur Westover, I never hear this word FM shoes in my life. So when you explain the meaning tonight I am horrified – you understand?'

Of course it was a rhetorical question; she was too wrapped up in her monologue to let me intervene. In fact, she seemed to be enjoying her little performance, like a contributor to some French chat show, talking earnestly, shaking her head a little and gesturing dramatically with her glasses in her hand.

'Oui, cette idée de 'Fuck-me shoes', c'est extraordinaire! Surtout d'un homme cultivé.'

'I've upset you.'

'Yes, it's true. Because when you first mentioned FM shoes, the other night – well, afterwards I thought about it and do you know what idea came into my innocent, naïve little mind?'

'No, tell me.'

'FM, I thought. What can this be, FM? Oh yes – I know: Finest Materials. Of course! Or even better, it could be Fashion Model shoes. You see, I had a positive interpretation in mind. But the vulgar truth you explain in your essay, I did not expect it from a man like you, not even from a *docteur*. Because it is the attitude of a man who judges women by their clothes, as sex-objects, and puts them in nasty little *catégories*. I mean to say, a *phallocrate*!'

'A what?'

She took half a dozen paces along by the window, gazing into space and clicking her fingers, barely audibly. Then she turned and just as purposefully paced back to the starting point. All the while that cocktail of emotions was swirling in my head – astonishment at her performance, nervousness, naturally, and yet also a certain frisson at being chastised by *la maîtresse de français*. But underlying them all there was scepticism: it didn't add up. That spiel about finest materials...

Then it hit me: the two of us were taking part in a game. And deep-down, I am sure we both knew it. A twisted little power game; one that, for all her apparent vulnerability and shockability, she had wanted from the outset. For with hindsight it is perfectly obvious that whatever I had written, however innocuous, Madame would have found something to object to; a reason to chastise me. Because that was her game plan.

She was standing by her attaché case, unfolding *le document*.

'I will remind you of the contract. Article 4 says: The two parties will behave in a professional manner of mutual respect, avoiding all references that are personal, sexual and... *dérogatoire*.' Steely look as she glanced up. 'But we cannot say that your attitude in your essay was respectful or acceptable, not to me and not to women in general.'

'Ah, well let me just –'

'So I think our professional relationship must be terminated immediately, according to Clause 8.' She began gathering up her papers into the case.

'Look – let's be rational about this. Firstly, I apologise unreservedly for any offence caused. But if I can explain, women's shoes are not my subject of choice. In fact, it was quite a stretch to even write a page on the subject – yes, I realise that's incredible, given all the medical papers I've had to write but there it is. So I had to broaden the subject a bit, take a slightly humorous, admittedly provocative approach. I thought you might see the funny side. But obviously, the whole thing has spectacularly backfired on me.'

By now she was in the doorway, looking resolute.

'Yes, it is unfortunate because you have put me in a very difficult situation.'

'Look, I'm sorry. But surely terminating the contract is pretty drastic. I mean, perhaps there's some alternative.'

'What do you mean?'

'Well, for example, I seem to remember another contractual clause… the one about accepting the authority and correction of the tutor. I mean, contractually speaking, you would be entitled to correct my unacceptable attitude. To rectify the transgression.'

Yes, that is how I phrased it: transgression.

'What are you suggesting, Michel?' Mystified look.

'Just thinking aloud… you could impose a financial penalty… or otherwise some other kind of corrective or disciplinary action. I don't know… Rap me with the ruler or give me five hundred lines on respect for women or whatever you like. For all I know, this may not be the first time you've had to resort to such measures…'

The bait was wafted in her direction but she avoided it.

'I do not discuss the affairs concerning other clients. However, I can assure you, if that situation could ever happen with another client, then I would certainly never give the discipline they asked for. A naughty child does not choose his punishment.'

'Of course not... So, have you decided? Are you going to reprimand me?'

'Is that what you want?'

The electric shock as our eyes met.

'Maybe we both want it.'

Silence for a few seconds, then the drumming of red fingernails on the door frame.

'OK, Michel...'

I have to hand it to you, Violette. You were masterly; ice-cool, coming back over to the table in those designer shoes and your sassy black dress. Opening the executive case, producing something small that I couldn't quite see. And that was the start of one of the strangest episodes in my life.

CHAPTER 8

Playing cards. French playing cards. Strange, unexpected and rather an anticlimax – although from the moment I saw them, I knew it wouldn't be a run-of-the-mill game. We started systematically, going through them, suit by suit, learning the names. 'Répétez, Michel…' And within a few minutes, I was able to glance at a king or a queen or an ace, and say *le roi, la dame, l'as…*

'Alors, on commence.'

She started laying the cards down in neat rows across the table – seven at the top, then six, five, four… then finally, turning the first card in each row face-up.

'On va jouer à la Patience. You say Patience, yes?'

'Yes…'

'What is the problem? Are you disappointed?'

'No, but I'm just wondering where this is…'

'So in the game you must say the French name of each card you pick up. OK?'

'Fine.'

She produced a rather insipid smile and pulled her chair round at right-angles to mine. 'So, Michel…' – carefully smoothing out the shiny black fabric over her knees – 'The time limit is fifteen minutes. We will play a short version. You must put the cards in *alternance*, red, black, red, and when you have completed one sequence, you will have won.'

'From the king to the ace, you mean?'

'Exactly. It is simple, yes?'

Well, it was easy enough at the start: nine of diamonds on to the ten of spades.

'Alors, Madame : Le neuf de carreau sur le dix de pique.'

'Bien, Michel. Tournez la carte – turn the new card underneath to replace the nine.'

So the game developed and I began building duos and trios of cards. Before long, up came the Jack of Diamonds. He made a threesome with the ten and the nine. But after that I was stymied.

'So, I'll take a card from the spare pile...'

'Un instant!' Her hand stopped mine halfway. 'Vous avez un gage.'

'Pardon?'

Enigmatic little smile from Madame.

'*Un gage*. Because you are blocked, before you take the next card, you must pay a penalty. *Un gage*, we say. So the first penalty will be... five pounds.'

Ah, I thought, so money comes into it. And in my wallet I found a tatty fiver.

'Voilà, Madame.'

'Merci.' She took it and put it the far side of her. 'Alors, continuez.'

Aided by the fresh card from the spare pile, I managed to set up a couple of new sequences and the Queen of Clubs appeared to help out the jack, the ten and the nine.

'La dame de trèfle.'

'Très bien.'

But then came the second stalemate and she couldn't conceal her pleasure.

'So, Michel, this time it will be fifty pounds.'

'Fifty quid! Bit steep, isn't it?'

'Don't dispute!' Frosty look. 'It is a logical progression.'

'I can see that. But what if I don't happen to have fifty quid on me?'

'Then you give me something else corresponding to the value.'

'Aha...'

'Of course, Michel, there is one rule you must obey.' I wondered what was coming as I saw her rather mischievous expression. 'You can give me anything you like that you can reach – but you are *not allowed* to leave your chair.'

Bizarre rule – strangely devoid, it seemed to me, of any logic. For had I been able to move, she could have had a very acceptable wine or even the expensive bottle of Calvados brought back from Normandy – but from my chair the choice was, to put it mildly, limited.

'You see, Michel, it is the Naughty chair.'

'Naughty chair!'

'Yes. Because you have been naughty.' Long, stern look. 'Broken the rules of la Maîtresse.'

'I see.'

'So for your *gage* what can you offer me?'

'Well, since I'm not allowed to move... it will have to be two things. First, my pen, not bad, worth about twenty-five.'

'All right...' She took it and gave it a cursory look. Obviously black lacquer was not nearly as exciting as her iridescent fountain pen.

'And secondly, my tie.'

'Oh – your tie!' Her eyes widened with what I thought was a flash of excitement. 'That's an original idea.'

She looked down and began squaring up the top row of cards with an apparent air of indifference while I set to unknotting the smooth silk.

'Voilà Madame. Une cravate rouge!'

'Oh yes, very good.' Brandishing it like a trophy! 'Italian and how you say racy red!'

'Indeed.'

Yes, she got the tie. A fitting offering of atonement, I guess, given my offending comments on sartorial style. Well, fitting in a twisted sort of way.

For the next few minutes I had my purple patch – managed to expand all the runs, shifting little piles here and there as she watched me. Three out of four of the kings now presided over a sequence, but by far the best was the impressive chain from the King of Hearts right down to the red three. I remember I was feeling a surge of optimism, that I would turn up the required cards and the absurd game would be over before I was bankrupt. In the event, it was only a matter of time until the run of luck ended and stalemate returned.

'So what now?'

Of course, I knew the score before she spoke.

'Five hundred pounds.'

'Five hundred – dammit! Well, I just don't see that happening. Not from this chair. There's nothing equating to that value.'

'No?' Quizzical look. 'Well, look behind you, Michel. Yes, that's right, the picture. What about it?'

'Boston lighthouse?'

'Yes. If you can touch it, we can include it. The rules allow.'

'Do they indeed? How very flexible of them! The only trouble is, I'm pretty attached to that picture, reminds me of a trip to New England several years ago. I particularly liked the old lighthouse with the distant skyscrapers behind.'

'Yes, I agree, it is elegant. I imagine it was quite expensive, this painting?'

'Well it wasn't cheap. I forget how much. But we can check it.' I twisted round, reaching up behind me beyond the point of comfort, to lift the picture off the hook. 'Ah: seven hundred dollars. A bit short of your total – although perhaps it's appreciated in value. Would it be acceptable to you?'

'Well, it is very nice.' Polite smile as she took the picture and laid it in the centre of the table. 'Thank you for that. Was it one of your favourite things?'

'One of them. By the way, what are you intending to do with my stuff – my forfeits, shall we call them?'

'Ah. Ça…' She had the look of the Sphinx. 'C'est mon petit secret.'

So – back to the spare pile, which yielded a useful card, enabling me to free up the system and uncover several new ones for the other runs, which were coming along nicely. A black two even emerged from its hiding place in the bottom row and with a grin I put it at the end of the magnificent King of Hearts chain. A moment of triumph before gridlock struck again.

'So,' I heard myself give a hollow laugh, 'forfeit time again.'

'Correct.'

'But it's so close! So bloody close! All I need is a red ace.'

'Ah yes, so close, Michel – *but* are you close enough?'

There was a glint in her eye. She was starting on the mind games now. Demoralise the opponent, make him doubt himself. Which was ridiculous because, unlike a bowler indulging in a bit of sledging to unnerve the batsman, her words could have no effect whatsoever on the ultimate outcome. Nonetheless, I felt the urge to talk things up.

'You know what? I have a feeling a red ace is sitting on the top of the spare pile, just waiting…'

I gave her a hard look, maximising the bluff.

'Oh – so you are feeling confident! But as you know, Michel, it's just a question of chance; if it is with you or with me…'

'Sure.'

'But you see, Michel, I am confident too! So confident, in fact, that I will give you a concession. You can look now, before the *gage*, just in case it's your wonderful ace.'

'And if it is?'

'You will win.'

'But if not?'

'You must pay me the penalty. In full. OK?'

'OK.'

'Allez, tournez!'

I began turning the card, mindful that the odds were stacked against me, fifteen to one, at least. But even so, in that split second I was trying to visualise a French Ace of Hearts or Diamonds: plenty of blank space with the small, red number 1 in each corner. But no. Far too much colour – a ruff, a cape, a plumed hat.

'Ha! Jack of Spades!'

'Le valet de pique. Répétez!'

'Le valet de pique… All dressed up and nowhere to go.'

'Oh, really? Are you sure he can't help you?' Sadistic little smile. 'Let's see…'

In the silence, I found myself staring at the dandified jack with his cocky face and he seemed to be sneering at me. But she, on the other hand, was cool and calm and in control, finger poised on her cheek, ready for her Oscar-winning performance.

'OK, so the black jack… he needs a red ten or a red queen, doesn't he? That is what we are looking for. Alors, voyons… le dix? Non, pas là, c'est noir… '

She continued her charade, infuriatingly slowly, looking

deliberately at every row, evaluating every possibility. Finally she looked up.

'No, you are right. There is nowhere for him. What a pity. Quel dommage.'

Quel dommage! That sickening tone of false sympathy!

'So, Michel…'

'Don't even bother saying it. I know full well…'

'You're angry, aren't you?' Her eyes were bright, triumphant. 'You want to stop, don't you? Hm? Don't you, Michel?'

'Well, you must admit, it's crazy; it's gone beyond a game into the realm of fantasy. I mean, you've got my prized American painting, my tie, my pen and you've got me glued to the chair like the naughty schoolboy – and still that's not enough.'

'OK – then you stop! Break your promise. Run away from the *gage*.' She gestured dramatically with her hands. 'Be the Englishman who doesn't like *le fair-play*. I am expecting it.'

She was loving it! Assassinating my character and in the process making herself feel superior. Le docteur anglais avec le duplex, le Porsche, le *'yote'* et cette attitude phallocrate. Et mon dieu, il était pathétique!

'Well, you're wrong.' I looked her straight in the eye. 'I don't break deals. Alors Madame, prononcez le gage.'

'Votre gage, docteur : cinq mille livres Sterling. Five thousand pounds.'

She announced it slowly and clearly with typical French drama – maybe she thought it would make more of an impression that way. But I was only half-listening; already racking my brains for ideas.

Five grand! What can she have for five grand? Or more to the point, what *can't* she have? Well, she won't be getting a big cheque off me, that's for sure. No. She's not going to take herself on a spree in Chelsea or Bond Street courtesy of my bank account. And she won't be getting the nineteenth-century microscope, my hard-won spoil from auction, sitting over there on the unit, just possibly within reach. No way!

'All right... you can have this.' Her look of amazement as I pushed back my cuff to reveal the Swiss masterpiece with the jewelled bezel. 'My Christmas present from Moira. Bought during a family ski-ing holiday, our last one together, actually. What do you think?'

She leaned over for the inspection.

'Hm, *chronomètre*,' she said, disdainfully 'voilà du snobisme!'

'You don't care for it?'

'No. I do not. It's too much, all this gold.'

'I see... But it cost well over 5k... so you should accept it as the penalty. Go on, take it.'

She took it from me in a matter-of-fact sort of way and began toying with the strap.

'Why do you wear this thing?'

'Well, it's undisputed in terms of craftsmanship and accuracy and I've always thought it looked elegant, I suppose.'

'You think so? To me it looks *vulgaire*. A symbol of *égotisme*. Because, believe me, I have seen the types who wear them: all the mon-ay but no soul.'

'Soulless. Is that what you're saying?'

'Yes, soul-less. *Sans âme*, we say in French. Remember this lovely little word, *l'âme*...' She leaned forward, suddenly very close, and spoke almost in a whisper. 'But, you know something, Michel? I think if we look hard enough, deep inside...' – I saw her pupils widening – 'maybe we find that, in fact, you have a soul.'

'Cheers. I'm deeply flattered.'

'Yes, you should be. Because some men, I assure you, they were born without one.'

'Is that a fact?'

She was still tantalisingly close, her perfume drifting over my face.

'Hundred per cent fact.'

She moved away again. 'So for your *gage* I will accept your watch but we need to modify the price because, after all, it is second hand! Therefore, to complete the forfeit, you need to give me one more object. Just a little thing, something symbolic.'

'Symbolic! Any suggestions?'

'That little thing there… on the pile of letters.'

'You want the carving?'

'Yes. Fetch it for me.'

'It's out of reach.'

'No! You can get it if you try. Lean over, Michel… Now pull the papers, from the edge… Allez! Tirez! Voilà.'

'You want this thing?'

'Show me.'

I remember brushing against her hand as I passed it to her. She cupped it in her palms, unduly cautious with a piece of basic English lime. Then she began turning it over and over in her hands.

'It's very smooth. A perfect kidney.'

'Would you pay a reasonable sum for it, if you saw it in a chic gallery?'

'Perhaps, if I really wanted it.'

'And do you want it, in full and final settlement of the last penalty?'

'Yes.'

'Then, take it! Go on – take the lot! And good luck, whatever you're going to do with it all.'

'Thank you very much.' She gave me a dazzling smile and

tossed the kidney gently into the air.

'Alors, Michel. C'est fini.'

She reached into her handbag, unfolding a small cloth tote bag printed with *Musée* something or other. The pen went in first, followed by the tie, the crumpled fiver, the kidney and the gleaming *chronomètre*. After that, she began collecting up the cards into their pack, all those colourful characters, silent witnesses to our strange ritual, disappearing from my sight. I was watching her in a daze as she tucked the flap into the packet.

'Bravo, Michel – you so nearly finished the sequence.'

'But I lost. Ultimately I lost.'

'Yes, you lost – but others could gain.'

'Others?'

'Yes, your things could be sold to support a good cause – maybe the victims of hunger or the AIDS orphans, yes? Imagine what your expensive Swiss watch could bring for them. And the elegant picture, your designer tie... What do you think?' She clicked the catches of her case.

'Very philanthropic.'

I got up to escort her downstairs, but with a firm 'Non!' she stopped me.

'You stay! Sit on your chair until I have gone. That is the rule, OK?'

'OK.'

'Alors, au revoir.'

She went into the hall by herself, clutching her case and the spoils of the game. From the foot of the stairs she called out: '*A la prochaine*' followed by a mischievous laugh. I heard the front door close, her heels on the path: c-lack, c-lack, c-lack, her car door opening and closing, then seconds later the ignition, slight revving, the wheels on the gravel and the engine fading.

Some fifteen minutes later, I suppose, after drinking an espresso and digesting the fact that the supposedly charming Violette had, like a confidence trickster, relieved me of at least five grand's worth of goods, and having checked my diary for our next lesson in early November, oh yes, and having scrawled a note to buy a cheap replacement watch first thing in the morning, I came down to lock the front door. And there was that extraordinary sight awaiting me:

Below the coat hooks, propped against the skirting board – Boston lighthouse! While close by was the small cotton bag, looking exactly the same: same pen, same tie, same old fiver, and, yes, incredibly, the same luxury watch. Why the hell didn't she take that – just slip it into her handbag? Why? Did she lose her nerve or feel a pang of conscience about taking valuables from a client? Or then again, wasn't it good enough for her? Too *vulgaire*! She must have laughed all the way home, imagining the look on my face! The sly little cow.

Still, all credit to her, it was a clever strategy, very clever – to drag everything out of me; no, not drag it, *persuade* it out of me, almost to the point where I could see the rationale for parting with it – and then throw it back at me. What a mind, to come up with that. Sharp, ingenious, mischievous, verging on the crooked…

And yet, for all the sharpness, not entirely focused or consistent. For as I picked up the bag, I suddenly noticed that the carving wasn't there. For some inexplicable reason, she'd taken that.

CHAPTER 9

We weren't due to meet for almost three weeks – no bad thing in view of the extraordinary climax to our fourth lesson. I imagine both of us were glad of the breathing space, both of us hoping that when we met again – *if* we met again – it would be business as usual. As if that bizarre game could be consigned to history!

Of course, I revisited it in my mind several times: trying to understand what had gone on and *why* I had allowed it to go on; and specifically why I had consented to the utterly absurd notion of the Naughty chair! What would a shrink have to say about that? As for Violette, clearly she was playing the role of *la maîtresse de classe*, but why? To indulge herself or me – or both? And the rationale of the game was beyond me. What on earth was the point of her insisting on my fulfilling every *gage*, of taking everything she wanted off me and spiriting it away out of my sight, only then (with one exception) to leave it? She had to be insane! Unless the sole objective was to prove a point: she could if she wanted.

In retrospect, however sketchy my understanding of the whole episode, it is pretty clear to me that what happened in those fifteen minutes was not just about la Maîtresse and l'étudiant; not even about Violette and Michel. No, what it was really about, as far as I can see, was Violette and the male sex in general. *Violette et les hommes*. Although whether that notion has ever occurred to her, I really could not say.

October seemed to flash by, largely uneventfully, with a couple of exceptions. Such as the sudden urge to drop in to the department after my scale and polish in the vicinity. '*Un caprice*' as Violette would say. And months on things looked much the same; scaffolding still up over the east wing; same 'temporary' mobile diagnostic unit, and a couple of scruffy individuals flouting the no-smoking rules by the door.

And yet, for all the familiarity, it felt strange strolling in to the main entrance; detecting the clinical smell and registering the multitude of signs, as if I had never entered the building in my life! Except that I then switched to autopilot and took the spur on the left leading down to Urology. Alison was busy typing but broke off to welcome me, insisting on hunting out my mug. I could see the correspondence in the folder awaiting someone's signature – someone's but not mine. We chatted for a couple of minutes while I had my coffee and got the low-down on the new 'drop dead gorgeous' nephrologist from eastern Europe. As for good old Abraham, he was in clinic, seeing the last patients, if I wanted to wait.

The unit looked exactly the same – well, except for the absence of my name plate on the door of consulting room one. As I hung around in the empty waiting bay, *my* door opened briefly to disgorge an elderly female. From within came the unmistakable sound of low mumblings into a Dictaphone. And when I knocked, who should be sitting in my chair but the young pretender in his loud pinstripes? Of course he didn't bother to get up when he saw me; just swivelled round and flashed a lightbulb smile my way.

'Michael… huh-huh-huh… how ya doing?'

How ya doing! As if we are best mates. Over the months I'd forgotten that extraordinary smug tone, somewhere between Eton and Essex, and the steely expression. Still, not wanting to be riled by a mere upstart, I did my best to keep things casual.

'Pretty good, thanks. Just been for a dental check-up, so I thought I'd look in, see how things are going.'

'Just dandy. In fact, you'll be delighted to know I've been whittling down your urge incontinence list.'

'Excellent.'

'Yes…' He was loosening his tie with his fleshy fingers. Maroon job with polka dots and what looked suspiciously like a blob of stale chocolate. 'Getting it all taped, if you'll excuse the pun. Eight per cent rise in through-put in the last six months.'

'Impressed you know the stats.' And I thought: but then, you've always seemed more like an endowment salesman than a clinician.

'Yes,' he rose abruptly from the chair, 'the key thing is sorting out the deserving cases from the timewasters draining NHS resources.'

Timewasters! Clever little *double-entendre*, that one, served up just for me. And predictably, he couldn't resist a jibe.

'By the way, how's the 'gardening' going? Cultivating a nice show of dahlias?' The little sniffling sneer to himself as he clipped his fountain pen onto his pocket. 'Well, it's been a long clinic… I'm off for sausages and mash.'

'Ah, good old canteen sausages. Miss those…'

'But Michael, you can have your leisurely *bruschettas* and *antipasti* any day you choose… Richmond, Putney, Chelsea – the world's your oyster…'

The perfunctory sweaty palm thrust in my direction, exerting undue pressure on my hand. 'Cheers Michael, I dare say you'll be back on board soon.'

'Let's hope so.'

At least he had the courtesy to usher me out ahead of him (I suppose on the basis of my being his elder, if not his better) and he mumbled something insincere about joining him in the canteen. Watching his stocky form shuffling down the corridor, I remember thinking: well, well, you jumped-up little jerk, if you're the future, God help the patients…

I barely had time to gather my thoughts when there was Abraham, fresh from clinic, delighted to see me. The feeling was mutual. So we headed for the canteen and he began filling me in on the latest non-achievable targets, the mountain of paperwork, and the failed third attempt to fix the theatre air-conditioning.

'Bet you can't wait to come back…'

Queuing up for the hot dishes, I saw my pinstriped colleague in the corner, stuffing his face. As we took our trays over to a spare table, there was the unmistakable cackle coming from the direction of the window, where the formidable Shagpile was doing her best to chat up a willowy junior doctor from the subcontinent.

'Ah, the delightful Sharon. See much of her, do you, Abraham?'

'Thankfully, no. My heart sinks if she's working on my list. However, most of the time she's hiding somewhere with a magazine, consuming chocolate bars, adding to her… how shall I say, considerable posterior.'

'Buffalo-esque, even.'

'As you say, buffalo-esque!'

'Although, lets be fair, Abraham; she could be taking exercise, nipping down the back stairs for a sly cigarette.'

'This is true. Or she could be busy entertaining the patients with her lavatorial humour.'

'Indeed, a rare talent, she has… amusing even, in small doses. You know, I once survived fifteen minutes of it at a nurses' party – ended up, slightly the worse for wear on a sofa next to her and she regaled me with her rich repertoire from genito-urinary medicine… Absolutely filthy! Then it got worse: she began draping herself over me. "Hey Mikey, you know what they say about bald men, ha-ha-ha!". Mortifying!'

'Did you get away?' The horror on his face!

'Yes, thank God. Like a praying mantis, she is…'

'But Mike, why on earth did you go? You must have known it was not your thing… with the juniors and physios and nurses young enough to be your daughter.'

'Yes, I know. What can I say, I guess I needed a bit of cheering up, turning fifty and getting the divorce finalised. So I thought why not? Have a couple of drinks, let my hair down (what there is of it!), go for a tacky evening. Well, makes a change from talking shop with my surgical colleagues over Noilly Prat.'

Shortly afterwards, while he was asking me about my news (or lack of it), there was the wonderful vision at the till: Leila, looking just as gorgeous as ever. She paid for her sandwich and was whisking past our table, when, to Abraham's surprise, I caught her arm.

'Michael Westover! What are you doing here?'

Same devastating smile, same plump red lips, same soft, seductive accent.

'Oh just looking in…'

'About time! We thought you must have emigrated or something.'

'No such luck.'

'Hey, you're looking good, though, much more relaxed.'

Those dark, dark eyes; so black the pupil merges into the iris.

'Any news on your return date?'

'Don't ask. There's no speeding these things up.'

'I guess not… So – what are you doing with yourself all day?'

'Reading my journals and research papers like a good boy.

Developing a couple of original ideas of my own... Apart from that, keeping an eye on the French property market. Oh and I'm having some private French lessons.'

'Impressive!' There was a hint of flirtatiousness in her voice. 'Ready to practise your charms on all those lovely French ladies...'

'I live in hope... And how's your family, your two... uh... daughters?'

'Oh, fine, fine. Nadia's joined her sister in secondary now. How about your son – Luke isn't it?' Sweeping her thick, black hair off her face; the gleam of her broad gold wedding ring.

'Yeah, Luke's fine. Started his second year at Leeds. Got himself a girlfriend, too.'

'Good. Well, I can't stop. Take care – drop by again.'

Another flash of her smile and she headed back to Paediatrics with her sandwich. So that was it, brief chat with the lovely Leila. A little top-up to keep me going for the next few months.

Apart from that encounter – how can I forget? – there was that exceptional Sunday in late October, a day of glorious, wall-to-wall sunshine, as if an Indian summer had packed itself into just eight hours. Blue sky, light breeze, twenty-one degrees – the perfect day for a sail. In fact, had I been free and had Edward been available, I would have been tempted to drive to Gosport and take *Entre Deux Mers* over to Ryde and back.

Still, it was a good day for the drive over the Hog's Back and down into rural Surrey for lunch with Chris and Anna and of course the new sproglet, Ollie. Amiable chap, rosy-cheeked, like a cheery little Henry VIII – packs a mean punch, too! Happy as Larry, tucking into his mini Sunday lunch of roast lamb and veg. As for Chris, I have to say, a return to fatherhood at fifty seemed to suit him. During our postprandial stroll around the village, he was the one proudly sporting the baby sling, evidently delighted with his lot: attractive wife, bouncing baby boy, eldest son at King's College... and of course, his shiny new professorship. At least he didn't gloat, obviously mindful of my less than perfect career at present. And I'm not sure if it was out of sympathy or generosity that, as I was leaving, he offered a free stay in their place at Saint Rémy de Provence. 'Any time – just say the word.'

The A3 London-bound was surprisingly clear and I must have got back around four. Just in time, like the rest of the inhabitants of Putney, to take a stroll on the Common. I stuck to the usual circuit of the pond and back. Exceptional birches, more golden than I've ever seen them, especially with the low sun, and the heather still had a tinge of colour. Of course, it wasn't exactly peaceful with all the dog-walkers, joggers, tricycles and push-chairs passing me by. Not to mention How-do-you-do Hilary coming up from behind in a skimpy top and shorts. 'Hi there, Mike... Fabulous day...' Then a brief chat – usual things: weather, slap-happy gardening contractors, the new couple at number eight, a run-down of forthcoming events at English National Opera should I happen to be interested... followed by the sting:

'So, who's the female with the black Volvo and the briefcase?'

Oh yes, she must have noticed Madame's crepuscular comings and goings, and indulged in a little speculation about the exploits inside number one!

'She's a private tutor. Occasionally comes to help me with my ailing French.'

'How fascinating! Good for you!'

I'm not sure if my explanation placated her or aroused a touch of jealousy. I suppose it's understandable; she looks out across the lawn and sees me – a free agent, professional, moderately presentable – and she sees herself, similar age, single, businesswoman, successful, new Merc convertible, so she thinks about the potential.

It was shortly after the encounter with Hilary on the way back from the pond that I made my find: the incredible zig-zag branch of birch, lying among the long, bleached grass. Slender, amazingly contorted by nature, just crying out for someone with a little imagination to take it home and convert it into something beautiful. So, birch in hand, applying some Pythagoras and taking the diagonal track back to the road, I began exploring the possibilities. With some careful carving, I could fully utilise the sinuous shape of the branch – create a slim female figure, about fifteen inches long, sitting up in a relaxed pose, knees bent, palms supporting her at the sides.

Yes, the idea was shaping up nicely when there was that altercation with the dogs on the path ahead near the brambles: the vigorous boxer bounding over to the little black spaniel. I remember the young student couple, seemingly oblivious at first, had some trouble getting the spaniel away – wouldn't respond to the guy at all. But the girl's whistle had the desired effect, as did her voice:

'Charlie! Charlie – viens, Charlie, vite!'

It was her! No mistaking the voice. *Ma maîtresse de français* out for a sunset walk on the Common. As she stood there, shaking the lead in her hand and chivvying the dim-witted dog along, even from my distance, I could make out the light brown hair under the brim of the hat. Oh yes, how fetching you looked, Violette – so lithe and youthful in your flimsy peasant skirt and the trendy flower-power hat. All of twenty-one from a distance! I could barely believe my eyes.

Naturally I allowed myself a stealthy look at him: long, lean, fair – the type that models leisurewear on Cape Cod. Walking tall in his grey denim jacket with *la petite Violette* by his side. Yes, an endearing sight they made, as they headed towards the main road, with the dog at their heels, and her arm strung through his.

The pathetic thing is that I thought a lot about her that evening. How could I possibly *not* have recognised her from behind, even from a dozen yards? Surely by now, after four sessions, I ought to have registered her height and neat little build, not to mention that distinctive, fluid walk. But then, to be fair, how was I to know she went in for young, hippy clothes at the weekend? In total contrast to her long linen suits and air-hostess outfits.

And then who the hell was he? Boyfriend? Husband? Maybe just a friend? Well, obviously a good friend – good enough to stroll along with arm-in-arm. Of course, he could have been her brother, over from France for the weekend. But no: since when do sisters and brothers link arms? Besides, if he was the brother, then where were his wife and the two nieces? What's more, he was too tall and fair for a typical Frenchman and the age didn't fit. What was he, late twenties, thirty at most? Considerably younger than Violette. In other words, in all probability, le toyboy!

Which was sufficient for me to take an instant dislike to the guy. Well, whoever he was, he had something on me; several things, actually. For a start, he had youth on his side. Youth and a full head of hair. And he was not at all bad-looking. But more than this, somehow he had managed to worm himself into the affections of the cool, discriminating, unpredictable Violette.

CHAPTER 10

There is no doubt that I was going to mention it at our next session, the following Wednesday. Just casually throw in some reference to the glorious Sunday, the world and his wife out for a stroll on the Common etc. Then wait for her to take the bait and say: '*Ah! quelle coincidence*' and shed some light on her male friend: '*Oh, c'était un ami.*' Or possibly '*C'était mon mari...*' But as it turned out, such plans were academic, thanks to her sudden sickness.

At least she had the grace to ring and give me a day's notice on the Tuesday morning. As soon as I heard the '*malheureusement*' in that husky voice over the line, I knew there would be a tale of woe. Poor Madame, sounding delicate and under par:

'Malheureusement, je suis enrhumée,' she said. *Enrhumée* – sounds so much more serious than merely a cold! But she was sincerely apologetic: 'Je suis désolée...'

'Oh non, ce n'est rien. Pas de problème.'

Obviously I was professional about it – asked what she was taking for her sore throat and the chesty cough, mentioned the possibility that she might be going down with a URTI. Then we spoke of rescheduling the session. Rescheduling: that was a joke! With her dance class (news to me) and other respective commitments we ruled out November. And December was a fiasco, at least on her part.

'Oh Michel, I am sorry.' She sounded a touch disingenuous.

'For the first week I have some work with a company. And then the next week, let me see...' She broke off and began mumbling several indistinguishable names. 'No, I am fully engaged with clients. Then we're going to the ballet, we never miss it. But after that... Ah mince, c'est impossible! You see, I must go to France to help my parents prepare for Christmas. You understand?'

'Well, you have to honour family arrangements.'

'Exactly, and now my father has the Parkinson's, he is very slow and my mother has to do so much...'

'Ah yes, I see. So in that case we'd better put the fifth session on ice.'

'On ice?'

'Yes, you know, postpone it until a later date.'

Possibly she detected the slight irritation I was feeling because she changed her tune and perked up a little.

'Attendez, Michel, j'ai une solution.' Une solution! That marvellous touch of Gallic drama. 'Nat-ur-al-ly you must keep practising your French because you are making so much progress... (flatterer!) So, for the next weeks, I will send you some exercises in *grammaire* and also some news articles from *Le Monde*. They will stretch you.'

'Excellent. I'll look forward to receiving those.'

'I will send them when I am better.'

'Thanks. And we're going to fix a date after Christmas? '

'But of course, one moment...' The old trick of flicking through her diary again but this time with the occasional cough for good measure.

'OK, Michel. I can propose eleventh January if it is good for you. For me this is perfect.'

Perfect! Only Violette would have the nerve to call that proposition, some two months away, 'perfect'. Still, what choice did I have? Eight o'clock on the eleventh it was. After that, with all the nonchalant charm I could muster, I wished her a speedy recovery and, for what it was worth, *joyeux Noël*.

So no French lessons until the New Year. Still, what the heck? Life goes on, I thought. And if you can't be bothered to meet me, Madame, I'll hop over La Manche and *parler* over there. Within a week or so I was doing just that, zipping off to Lille with Edward and Jill by Eurostar. First class treat for my birthday. And what an excellent day it was – champagne en route, blue skies and golden poplars flashing by, and a late morning stroll through the old town to Edward's favourite restaurant. *Filet de bœuf au coulis de foie gras, plateau de fromages, café…*

After lunch we headed for the splendid Palais des Beaux Arts. A whole host of famous names to be seen but of all of them, Rubens shone the brightest. I remember the three of us were awe-struck by that canvas of the ghostly Christ being taken down from the cross. Then there was Monet's Houses of Parliament in purple fog, apparently painted from a room in St. Thomas's.

Then to round off our visit – what else but le shopping? Our attention was caught by those flamboyant shirts in the window display with the sign: *Promotion sur les chemises*. So we were tempted inside for a closer look – luxurious pure silk, obviously designed for Continental men who do bright shirts so much better than we Brits. Of course, in true brotherly style, Edward grabbed the deep red one before I had a chance.

'Oh, did you want the maroon?' That disingenuous tone I know so well. 'Shame there isn't another.'

'No, you take it. Finders keepers!'

The young sales girl obviously overheard.

'Messieurs, je peux vous aider?'

She was petite but studious-looking with black, rectangular glasses. It was hard to know which term to use: Mademoiselle or Madame.

'Ah oui, Madame, je cherche une chemise...' And I launched in with my bit about colours and sizes and within half a minute she returned, profusely apologising for the lack of maroon but bearing the alternative in the rich gold.

'Une très belle chemise, fabriquée en Italie. Vous voulez l'essayer?'

'Oui.'

Edward emerged from the fitting room, looking very pleased with himself.

'So that's settled. I'll take the red. Now let's see Michael in the mustard.'

'Mustard? You know, Ed, your colour sense is appalling.'

'Well, mustard, bronze... whatever, you've got a nice shirt there. Thirty per cent off, too.'

I wasn't convinced. Even with the reduction, it was still pricey. Besides, when would I need a gold silk shirt? However, quality speaks for itself – heavy cloth, excellent cut and, to my delight, a perfect fit. It certainly got the thumbs-up from Jill:

'You look fantastic! Doesn't he, Edward, in the gold? Really brings out his hazel eyes.'

So, clutching our spoils, Ed and I went with Mademoiselle to the cash desk.

'C'est décidé?'

'Oui. Vous acceptez les cartes de crédit?'

'Bien sûr.' She began wrapping my shirt in tissue. 'Vous êtes anglais, Monsieur?'

'Oui.'

'Mais vous parlez *bien* français.'

'Merci.'

A delightful smile just for me as she handed over my carrier, wishing me *bonne soirée*.

On the homeward run we sat chatting excitedly, passing through dark, invisible Flanders, surrounded by our bags of pâté and cheeses, beer, art calendars, perfume, magazines, books, maps and of course, the extravagant shirts.

At St Pancras we parted company, Ed and Jill heading north, and me south for Waterloo. I remember feeling acutely aware of my flash carrier bags as I passed some unsavoury characters in the subways of the underground, eager to reach the platform and merge in with the crowd. Fat chance – around the corner was the young guy slumped on the floor, dripping blood, with his fellow citizens passing by – as if they had seen it all before or had suddenly all developed tunnel vision. What was I going to do – ignore him, conveniently forget my pledge of service to humanity?

He was conscious, staring blankly at the floor. I can see him now – pale, skinny with bright red hair, similar in age to Luke. I remember his dazed, apprehensive expression as I bent down to speak to him, not sure if I were friend or foe. But he seemed lucid enough, able to tell me his name: Alistair. However, as for my follow-up question about the cause of his head injury, he was less forthcoming.

'What's it to you, anyway?' As well as the dejected tone, the Scottish accent was obvious.

'I'm a doctor – just wanted to see if you needed any help.'

'Doctor?' He was obviously bemused by all the shopping bags.

'Off duty. Just been on a day-trip by Eurostar.'

'Oh that thing.' He looked singularly unimpressed.

'So, Alistair, can I take a look at your head?'

'If you want.'

I dispensed with the bags, propping them up against the tiled wall next to him, and he sat up for me, raising his head while I assessed the wound above his left eye.

'So, how long have you been in this state?'

'Not sure… few minutes.'

'Have you felt dizzy, faint or lost consciousness?'

'No. But my head stings like hell.'

'I bet. Although luckily, it's not a deep cut – shouldn't need stitches. Bit of antiseptic should do, if you have any at home. Although there's a V-shaped nick there, obviously caused by something sharp.'

He winced as he wiped some blood from his eyebrow and stared at it on his finger.

'That'll be his fucking ring.'

'Whose ring?'

'The bastard who smacked me in the face.'

'Where?'

'Back there on the escalator… I'd just left my mate after a couple of drinks, keeping myself to myself, and this group of guys comes down behind me, really loud, aggressive types, you know. And the big guy goes past and shouts: "Fucking ginger". So I say something and next thing he turns round: smack! His fist on my head.'

Words of wisdom came to mind, the ones I say to Luke: Don't answer back. Don't get involved. Just walk away. But they would have gone down like a lead balloon.

'Sickening… Where did they go?'

'Down there to the platform. They'll be away now for sure.'

'Well, in the circumstances that's no bad thing. Anyway shall I clean you up a bit? Make you more presentable?'

He nodded, watching me open my bottle of water and moisten the improvised pad of tissues. As I started cleaning the periphery of the wound, I decided to risk my bright idea.

'You know, you could report it to the police.'

He looked at me as if I were insane!

'What's the point? They'd do fuck all.'

'Look, if you want, I'll make a statement with you. Say when I found you and the condition of the wound.'

'Na. Forget it. I just want to be home.'

'Well, if you're sure.'

'Yeah.'

He grabbed several swigs of water and we stayed a couple of minutes more, while I checked his vision. Then he got to his feet and we went down to the platform. Within half a minute the train came. During the journey we spoke little. I could have asked, as the train rattled along, about his home, if there would be someone waiting for his return. But it wasn't my place to start probing. By the time I had to change tube trains, he seemed all right. So I left him, quiet but nonetheless grateful, heading home, and I hoped that the rest of his journey would be uneventful.

After the interlude of Lille, normal service was resumed in Putney; days and days of November drizzle. I laid low and got on with the woodcarving in the studio. After its 'fast-track' seasoning in the airing cupboard, the sinuous piece of birch seemed in a perfectly workable condition. Once stripped of the bark and prepared with the fret saw, the wood was beautiful: pale and even-grained, perfect for the seductive sylph in my mind. After a couple of weeks, she was taking shape: sleek calves and thighs, nipped in waist, beautiful arms and shoulders. But as for her face and hands – they were the swine. So I abandoned her in disgust on the workbench.

Come early December the Christmas cards and drinks invitations started arriving. I remember casting a critical eye over my wardrobe (very unexciting bar the shirt) and then casting an equally critical eye over the guy in the mirror: Michael Westover, MS, FRCS (Urol), 53, resplendent in his Calvin Kleins. Reasonable chest and shoulders, athletic legs but an undeniably porky midriff – just awaiting the imminent onslaught of cheese and wine, mince pies and chocolates, to say nothing of turkey and Christmas pud.

So that was the catalyst for the fitness regime. Up at six thirty and in the leisure pool by seven, pushing myself to the limit: seventeen lengths today, nineteen tomorrow… and so on till I peaked at thirty. Nothing, of course, on that incredible Olympic Helga in her go-faster-stripes, notching up her daily mile – but then she was a different species! Still, persistence pays; after several weeks the pounds were dropping off, the abdominal muscles were firming up and I felt decidedly bullish.

Luke even noticed when he arrived on the 23rd. Just in time to dash out for a last-minute blue spruce, get the thing home and haul it upstairs into the living room. He was happy to do the lot: throw on the tinsel, fix the lights, wrap some foil around the pot. That evening we had a take-away in the festive glow and downed a couple of beers while delving into my rock archives – Cream, Hendrix, Purple, Floyd and Led Zep.

On Christmas Eve, having fled the heaving King's Road, we set up the chessboard. Just like old times, gritting our teeth, each of us determined to outwit the other. But he'd learnt new tricks that term from the university chess club and within forty minutes it was all over. 'Yes!' Punching the air! The first time in his life that Luke beat his dad. But the return match in the evening was a close-run thing; in fact, I was within an ace of capturing his queen when the phone rang.

Moira! Quick advance call to wish us both happy Christmas

and to share the news. Well, what could I say? Congratulations, obviously, and the best of luck to her and John. Did I feel the slightest pang at the prospect of my ex-wife being betrothed to another? Maybe. But only a slight one.

The subject came up inevitably over Christmas lunch at Edward and Jill's. Whole barrage of questions directed at me from Jill and the twin girls, while Edward, resplendent in his maroon silk shirt, was engrossed in carving. Who's John? Does he have kids? How did they meet? Would I go if invited? That was the only question I could answer!

After that, thankfully, I was allowed to become acquainted with the velvety Château Margaux waiting in my glass. While the six of us were indulging in our turkey and Christmas pudding, I thought about Madame celebrating in Normandy – what would she be having? Champagne and local oysters, followed by duck or goose or even lobster, and probably one of those French Christmas logs for dessert. Plus a drop or two of Calva. Yes, a jolly festive time with Maman, Papa and all the family. And quite possibly le toyboy.

Boxing Day was the usual; a walk by St. Alban's abbey and then back home for a soporific afternoon. We divided into two camps: Luke and the girls upstairs with their iPods, and the three of us downstairs, watching TV or trying out my Christmas set of French CDs (ideal, except for the announcer cutting in too fast during the practice part before you could even think of the *français*, let alone splutter it out!)

But the excitement came in the evening when we returned to Putney: the small, white envelope waiting on the doormat. Luke was the one to pick it up and thrust it casually my way. In one corner was Hilary's scrawled message about the incompetent postman. It was franked 15 December and the address was written in an unfamiliar hand: Doctor Westover and what looked like 7 Monterey Drive. A late card from an ex-patient, I thought. But when I opened the envelope, was I surprised to find that alpine snow-scene overprinted in silver with *bonne année* – and to see the familiar loopy handwriting:

Cher Michel
Une petite invitation à notre réveillon pour la
Saint-Sylvestre, le 31 décembre à partir de 20h30.
En espérant avoir le plaisir de vous revoir,
Bien cordialement,
Violette

Adresse: 11 Sweetbriar Court, Wimbledon

I was cock-a-hoop, like a kid! Called Luke back from the top of the stairs.

'Hey – get this. Your father's invited to a French New Year's Eve party! *Un réveillon*, no less.'

'Cool.'

'It's better than cool. It's decidedly classy... I mean, how could I possibly refuse?'

So I got on the phone straightaway, rehearsing my lines while I dialled: Bonsoir, Violette, c'est Michel. Merci pour la très gentille invitation. J'accepte avec grand plaisir.

'Hel-lo.' Young male, educated voice.

'Ah, hello... could I speak to Violette please?'

'No... I'm afraid she's in the bath. Can I help?'

Pleasant but slightly precious. I could see him at the end of the line, taut and blond, her pretty toy boy.

'Yes. It's Michael Westover here – one of Violette's private students. Could you pass on my thanks for the invitation and say I'd be delighted to come.'

'Of course, she'll be thrilled. We're both looking forward to it enormously – it's our third one actually. We like to put together a cosy little do, something a bit different.'

How very cosy for you both...

'Can I bring some wine, champagne?'

'Oh, no need honestly – unless you really want to. By the way, hot tip: we do a wicked French buffet.'

'Terrific! So I'll look forward to seeing you – and Violette of course – on the thirty-first.'

And I did look forward to it, but not wholeheartedly. On the one hand it sounded appealing enough: speaking French with Violette, sampling the food, swigging a nice Claret or Burgundy (if I was lucky) and seeing in the New Year *à la française* – yes, all very pleasant. But then *he* would obviously come into it, which could be irritating or downright nauseating. And then presumably there would be various other students or francophiles who might or might not be my scene. And unless she'd brought over a crowd of authentic French friends to liven it up (which seemed unlikely as they'd be celebrating over there) it could all be a bit too cosy and suburban for my liking. Still there was one certainty, however it turned out: at least it would be different and, without a shadow of a doubt, *très civilisé*.

CHAPTER 11

Sweetbriar Court: secluded haven of suburban gentility with its Tudor rose mouldings, diamond-leaded panes and neat front gardens – quite irresistible to a French woman with an eye for 'old English' charm. But for all the kitsch there was a certain festive cosiness about the dozen or so semis and their glowing windows, especially number eleven with the white lights strung over the porch and through the ivy.

I recall the sense of anticipation, as I walked up the frosty path past the Volvo and a 'cool' new mini, glimpsing a cluster of indistinct figures behind the windows – realising what lay ahead could be delightful or positively excruciating, but never imagining that the evening would bring me an extraordinary insight into Violette, as I had never seen her before.

Somehow I hadn't counted on being greeted by the toy boy, yet there he was, long and lean, making a style statement in his Seventies circles print shirt. Nothing but hospitable, though, with his warm handshake and the 'Hi, I'm Simon – you must be Michael' intro. And I have to say, far from a wary rival, he was the gracious host, holding my gifts to enable me to shed my jacket, then going in search of the hostess while I waited in the hall, catching the hum of conversation plus the strains of *La Vie en Rose* emerging from the door to my left.

Of course, I was apprehensive – well, after all, it was our first meeting since the game. I wondered how she would react to me after so many weeks – would she be cool, over-effusive or business-like? A sudden waft of warm seafood (prawns I assumed) and she appeared from the kitchen: la maîtresse de maison.

'Ah, Michel!'

Stunning vision in a floaty black dress, approaching with theatrically parted arms. And – result! – the honour of a French *bise*, one kiss on each side, so skilfully done, I barely felt the brush of her cheek. Then she stood back, looking approvingly at my silk shirt from Brussels.

'Mais, Michel, vous êtes en pleine forme, vraiment. Et la belle chemise…'

'Merci. Et Violette, vous êtes très chic… éblouissante!'

Yes, dazzling she most certainly was in that seductive dress with the semi-transparent side panels. Not surprisingly, the Dom Perignon went down well, but I hadn't imagined she would be so thrilled with my simple offering of the white tulips, for as she passed the gifts over to Simon, she had far more to say about the flowers than the champagne.

She led me through to meet the other guests. I remember it was a long room with flock wallpaper, a couple of sofas, one of them vivid pink, and some customized antique-effect chairs in bright patchwork and velvet. At the far end a large baroque-style mirror dominated one wall. I suppose about fifteen people were milling around, chatting until Madame commanded attention with a clap of her hands.

'Mesdames et Messieurs, je vous présente Docteur Michael Westover… ou tout simplement, Michel.' After that gracious introduction, she reeled off the names of the sea of pleasant faces, a good half of whom I barely spoke to all evening. It was my lot to be standing next to the two grey-haired, ruddy-faced francophiles, the rotund 'Guillaume' and angular 'Edouard'. Boy, could they talk – especially Edouard, his voice booming out across the room, above the café songs, to deliver his monologue in annoyingly good French: the tale of his beloved *manoir* in the Dordogne, the team of local builders slaving away on the restoration, his amicable dealings with Monsieur le Maire.

'Alors...' – I remembered my tutor's use of alors as a casual but impressive introduction – 'Alors Edouard, vous recommandez la vie en France?'

'Mais oui, la qualité de la vie est infiniment supérieure à l'Angleterre...' Self-satisfied smile and a gulp of his *apéritif*. Then he began waxing lyrical over the marvellous fresh produce, the traffic-free roads, the long, hot summers... *Merveilleux, merveilleux*. Eventually, he was good enough to extend the conversation to the two of us.

'Et vous Michel, vous avez une résidence secondaire?'

'Non, mais j'ai l'intention...'

'Quelle région?'

'Provence...' No doubt I produced all the clichés – small character house with shutters, decent plot of land, maybe a vine, friendly natives who would invite me round for a pastis or whatever. At that point Violette returned, escorting the leggy Sloane Ranger in the skimpy dress with the rock of an engagement ring.

'Michel, let me present our guest from Ful-ham, Fyon-ah.'

It sounded so endearingly French, so different from the hard, clipped English tones of the young bond dealer herself. But for all the rah-rah and City talk, Fiona was pleasant enough company over the *apéritif* graciously handed to us both by our hostess:

'Ah, Violette's scrummy Pommeau! Santé, Michel!'

'Santé!'

It was a shade sweet for my taste, like a cider-sherry hybrid, but a pleasant enough lubricant while Fiona and I chatted about our respective professions, Paris, holidays... Then we got onto the amazing Millau viaduct – '*le pont flottant*' as she quaintly called it. At which point Edouard stuck his oar in.

'Oui, oui, le Viaduc de Millau, voilà un exemple de l'esprit innovateur et entrepreneurial des grands projets français. C'est magnifique.'

Mercifully, Simon called us through then for the buffet. I remember filing through the warm, aromatic kitchen behind Guillaume and into the conservatory with the tall, white Christmas tree, laden with purple baubles and sequinned robins. Awaiting us were two mouth-watering visions: the impressive array of starters laid out on the long table and, beyond them, Madame herself, lapping up people's oohs and aahs, every inch the radiant hostess:

'So for the *entrées* we have scallops: *Saint-Jacques au Calvados*, or there is ham terrine with parsley, which we call *jambon persillé*. Or chicken liver mousse with champagne... and we have *crudités à la mayonnaise*. Help yourselves and afterwards Simon will assist you with your drinks.'

Guillaume was not shy in scooping out a generous portion of the pink and green terrine onto his plate.

'Ah, *le jambon persillé*, délicieux!' A kiss of his fingertips à la French chef. 'Madame, tell us your secret recipe.'

'It's very simple. You cook the ham very tenderly with white wine, vegetables... Then you put layers of the ham and the fresh parsley and you let it become a delicious *gelée* in the refrigerator. Will you try some, Michel?'

Her pretty eyes imploring me.

'Well, it looks quite superb... but I've already set my heart on those scallops.'

'But then you must have both!'

'Merci Madame. C'est magnifique.'

So with my double starter, I went away happy as a sand-boy! Piaf was still bleating away in the living room and I decided to bag myself a space on the cream sofa, on the basis of it not being shocking pink. Oh Violette, your *coquilles St-Jacques*, sweet and delicious they were with the bright coral roe and the rich Calvados. After a few moments of bliss, Guillaume joined me for some rather limited conversation. He spoke between mouthfuls, his face plump and pink as a suckling pig.

'D'you know, doctor, last Easter we stayed at a super mini château in the Loire… Marvellous food. And guess what I had every night as an *entrée*?'

'*Jambon persillé*?'

'Exactement, docteur.'

After that it was the saga of his bradycardia, but just when he was asking for advice, Fiona joined us, slotting herself between us, her knees almost touching mine. We began comparing notes. Quite obviously, she was one of Madame's high flyers:

'Yes – we've been reading several classics this year – Proust, Camus, Molière. How about you, Michael?'

'Nothing so impressive. But the other week she gave me an absolute swine of a listening exercise from French radio: la Bourse de Paris.'

'Ah, she likes to keep you on your toes. You never know quite what she'll dream up next.'

'Too right! Take the contract…'

'Contract?' Look of utter amazement.

'Yes, contract. Or should I say, *l'accord*?'

'L'accord?' Still looking at me, nonplussed.

'Ah, I take it you don't have one?'

'Heavens, no! Whoever heard of contracts for private tuition? Have you got one, William? A contract…?'

But Guillaume was engaged in conversation with the plump woman in the gaudy dress so Fiona and I continued our conversation *à deux*, in hushed tones naturally.

'So Michael, I'm dying to know: what sort of things does it cover, your *accord*?'

'Oh, pretty standard stuff. Terms of payment, cancellations, copyright of materials…'

'Ah, nothing very interesting then.' Definite hint of disappointment in her voice.

'Well actually, there are a couple of, let's say *unusual* clauses on attitude and correction.'

'Correction? What on earth does she mean by that?'

'Million dollar question! You'd assume it implies grammatical correction unless she was meaning something more *risqué*…'

A sudden waft of air – Violette breezing past, right on cue. I found myself drying up like a naughty schoolboy overheard in assembly. But not only did she hear – she clearly disapproved, judging by the filthy look flung my way from across the room. A short, sharp dagger of a look with an unequivocal message: the terms of our contract were strictly confidential, between the two of us; between la Maîtresse and her student. In the ensuing seconds, I wondered if she might produce some withering remark in front of everyone to pay me back for my indiscretion. But no – cool and efficient, she took off Piaf and started sifting through the CDs. After which she gave me a charming smile as she announced the song.

'Voici une belle chanson de Jean Sablon: *Prenez garde au grand méchant loup*.'

It was a jolly Thirties number which, as some perceptive soul commented, was indeed to the tune of 'Who's afraid of the big bad wolf'. Guillaume was obviously a connoisseur:

'Ah, l'inimitable Jean Sablon. Le Bing Crosby français.'

I remember people stopped chatting to listen to the witty lyrics, while two of the women bravely tried to join in with the chorus. Violette then disappeared with Simon in the direction of the kitchen and its tempting, rich aromas. Just a couple of minutes later we went through for the presentation of the duck with cherries, John Dory with herbs, and the memorable rabbit.

'What would you like, Michel?' Her hand, trailing over an oven dish, flashing a pink gemstone ring.

It was going to be the fish, of course. But then, when did I ever see humble rabbit on offer at a party? Rabbit in golden cider. She seemed keen to persuade me.

'It's delicious. Une *spécialité normande!*'

'Alors, naturellement je voudrais le lapin!'

She beamed, serving me a sizeable portion, and I returned to the living room knowing my choice had pleased her and, with any luck, atoned for my earlier misdemeanour.

Since the City lawyer type in the OTT waistcoat had pinched the space next to Fiona (I recall his every sentence started 'Yes, no, indeed…') I ended up on the bright pink sofa next to the GP, Doctor Khan. Of course we exchanged a few words on our respective roles within the health service and then he began raving over his John Dory, almost as good, he said, as the hilsha of his native Bangladesh.

'Yes, it is a pleasure to find such a fish on offer. But Madame Lorance always produces marvellous food on such occasions. And she is such a *charming* tutor. She is regularly coming to our house, once a week, for French study, which I always look forward to immensely.'

'I'm sure. You must be pretty fluent, I'd imagine.'

'No, alas, my conversational French leaves much to be desired. Truth to tell, I murder the language. I say this to

Madame and she laughs and says I speak French *comme une vache espagnole*!'

'That's a good one!'

'Whereas you, Michael, I have been noticing, you speak very well indeed. Vous parlez très bien.'

'Ah non, non! Je suis médiocre.'

'Médiocre! Well, if you are médiocre, then I must surely be diabolique – if one can say this.'

I was only half concentrating, noticing Violette in the doorway, clutching her plate and wine glass, gazing across the crowded room.

My gallant colleague sprang to his feet.

'Madame, please come and join us.'

She slipped in between us and I felt the swish of her dress across my hand before she brought it into line.

'La rose…' I joked.

She laughed politely. 'So, gentlemen, you have been talking French?'

'Yes, and I have discovered Michael is much better than me.'

She turned to protest to the doctor. 'Oh no! Ac-tu-al-ly, Docteur Khan, you are one of my most dedicated students. Tell Michel about your project.'

'Well, Michael…' He had to lean forward to look at me, past Violette. 'With the assistance of our delightful professeur, I am attempting to read *Madame Bovary* in the original French.'

'Isn't that wonderful, Michel?' Glancing at me, as she reached for her glass on the table.

'Very impressive. Actually, I remember the TV serial years ago now…' Memories of Moira on the sofa, rapt and monosyllabic. 'About a doctor's wife and her extra-marital affairs, as I recall.'

Beam of approval from Madame.

'That's right, Michel. The novel is an *analyse* of the

desperation of a woman in a boring marriage with a country doctor. *La médiocrité et l'ennui…'*

I remember that awkward pause, which Doctor Khan and I plugged with our respective compliments on her food. She smiled, her plate of salad perched on her lap, then continued:

'But I also learn from my students. For example, Docteur Khan taught me something very interesting, didn't you?'

He looked nonplussed until she playfully tapped her knee.

'Ah yes, *genou*!' My medical colleague wagging his finger, his eyes flashing. 'A little word of great significance, n'est-ce pas, Madame Lorance?'

I caught the exchange of glances between them.

'Oh – what kind of significance?'

The ludicrous visions that sprang to mind… The chivalrous doctor in the privacy of his study, lifting Madame's skirt to tend to an injured patella: 'Permettez moi d'examiner votre genou.' Or Violette, unable to contain herself, casting *L'art de conjuguer* aside and throwing herself on the good doctor's knee! After all, he might be her type: impeccably dressed, glossy-haired yet elegantly greying at the temples, and well spoken with delightful Asian flourishes here and there.

'Well, Michael,' he smiled, 'In Bangla and Sanskrit we have for the knee the word *janu* – very like the French *genou*, the explanation being that both words – *genou, janu* – are deriving from languages belonging to the Indo-European group.'

'Oh yes, Docteur Khan!' Madame la Professeur in overdrive, leaning towards him, while I had the pleasure of her back and a waft of perfume. 'We had such a *fascinating* conversation about etymology, didn't we? And you told me so many other things. I must say, this brings a very exciting dimension to language-learning.'

She was being so utterly charming to him and, pleasant as he was, I was beginning to feel distinctly *de trop* – the also-ran in the mutual admiration stakes.

'Would you excuse me for a couple of minutes?'

'But of course, Michel.'

I located the bathroom easily enough but it was occupied. So what choice did I have but to loiter on the landing? A few feet away from the snuffling nose of the spaniel, trapped the other side of the rear bedroom door. But the front bedroom was on open view – an inviting, softly lit room with the double bed and the silky quilt, onto which she'd flung the hairdryer, not to mention the little black bra. While on the bedside cabinet was a French novel. The open top drawer allowed a glimpse of her anti-depressants, and – lo and behold – my kidney carving.

The bolt clicked on the bathroom door and Guillaume emerged but not before I'd scrambled back on to the landing, seemingly intrigued by the row of foreign dictionaries in the bookcase and the back issues of *Vogue*.

'Ah, ah Monsieur le docteur! Vous amusez beaucoup?'

'Oui, c'est une soirée magnifique.'

'Oui, oui, magnifique….'

The bathroom was immaculate. French soap, soft towels and the array of designer shower gels and lotions – for him and her. What else? A few seashells in a bowl and, floating in the bin, the crumpled tissue with the pink lipstick kiss. Sprucing myself up, I heard a few barks from next door followed by Violette's soothing tones, and when I came out, there she was in her bedroom, clutching a packet of antacid tablets.

'Oh, Violette. Are you OK there?'

'Yes. It is just indigestion.'

'Something rich you've eaten?' I ventured over the threshold, into *la chambre*.

'It's nothing. I rush around too much today. Anyway, the pain will go now I have taken my pill.'

'Where's the pain: in your stomach... the bowel?'

'The stomach, I think.'

'What sort of pain? Gnawing, burning, griping?'

'Don't ask me, it's just the stomach ache; it will go.'

'Have you seen your doctor about it?'

'No. But if I have the need, Michel, I will see my *généraliste*.' Her tone was a little irritated. 'Or otherwise I just go to the pharmacie or the homoeopath. But I don't need to consult a surgeon for *dyspepsie*!'

'I see. Well, if you change your mind, I'm happy to –'

'Anyway, you surgeons,' – nervous little laugh – 'you fix people, like you are *mécaniciens*. But because I am not broken down like an old *bagnole*, I don't need a *mécanicien*! Do I?' Her eyes glinted, mischievously.

'Evidently not. So we'll just assume it's a touch of IBS then. You seem to have a sensitive gut.'

'Yes. That must be the explanation.'

Slightly edgily, she whisked the black bra off the quilt and into a drawer. I noticed the smart black mobile on the far side of the bed, quite unlike her usual silver one. Simon's presumably.

She took a lipstick from her bag, flicked out a tiny circular mirror from the base of the tube, and started painting her lips with supreme skill. At which point my thoughts strayed with the crazy idea: Michael Westover conducting the palpation of Madame's abdomen – purely as a favour, of course. And she would be compliant, lying back on her quilt, lifting the flimsy black dress over her ribs, allowing me to explore her soft skin for any hint of rebound tenderness or organomegaly...

She clicked the tube, the magic mirror vanished.

'That's a 007 lipstick you've got there!'

Puzzled look. 'No… it's Guerlain.'

Back downstairs, Simon was on dessert duty in the conservatory, presiding over yet more temptations:

'So, Michael, what can I get you? Pears in red wine or Violette's yummy crème caramel? Or some of my dual chocolate mousse?'

His eyes, unnervingly blue and piercing; the kind of eyes some women find irresistible. Quite possibly, women such as Violette. Then again, maybe the startling blue was all down to the wonders of coloured contacts.

The room was very warm now with the buzz of relaxed conversation. Only Guillaume and Edouard were sticking to French, with the occasional contribution from Doctor Khan. As for Violette, I noticed her chatting with the family of the teenage schoolgirl, her star pupil apparently. I brushed past, to the space by the alcove with the music collection. Jacques Brel, Georges Brassens, Serge somebody. Who else was there? Diana Ross, Donna Summer, various disco hits, and a cool type called Doc Gynéco, incongruously nestling alongside Chopin.

While I was finishing dessert, Simon came over and we exchanged a few niceties about his dual chocolate mousse. I recall noticing Violette helping the little blonde sister of the schoolgirl onto a dining chair and placing a large serviette on her lap, followed by a bowl of ice cream. After which she stood, watching the little cherub eating her treat, and chatting in French to the big sister. Then Edouard caught my eye, red-faced, holding his bread plate below his chin, spectacularly demolishing a wedge of camembert in one.

I suppose it was the prospect of some cheese and wine that tempted me out into the conservatory. And had I not been there, I would never have heard that revealing conversation between Fiona and the hostess of the *soirée*.

CHAPTER 12

I hadn't intended to stay long – but the wicker chair by the French doors was inviting, conveniently screened from civilisation by the extravagant white Christmas tree. So there it was, a few minutes later, as I was savouring the soft, mellow Chaûmes, and admiring the considerable effort invested in attaching all those baubles, that I heard Violette's voice, drifting through. She and Fiona, talking in the kitchen...

'Fabulous dress... that *lace*... Is it French?'

'No, it was from Italy. But you're right, it could be French. My wedding dress was lace – white of course.'

So they began talking weddings... Riveting! Not that I could hear everything over the coffee machine but my ears pricked up when I caught the words *mariage civile*, definitely spoken by Violette. Then there were murmurings about who wanted caff and decaff and the next thing I knew, they were talking about him: *le mari*.

'Hervé? Oh, he was an architect. We met at my cousin's wedding in Bordeaux. The big impression! Good-looking, intelligent, full of charm...'

'Ideal!'

'Mm, I thought so. But maybe it's unlucky to meet your future husband at a wedding.'

It was intriguing sitting there, piecing together parts of the jigsaw. She was an English teacher in a *lycée*, a schoolmistress no less! Young, enthusiastic, optimistic. And the two of them were happy enough in the early years at least. Nice house by the sound of it – Scandinavian style (his design), plenty of glass, solar panels.

'So tell me, what went wrong?'

'Oh, I made the mistake to talk seriously about children. We were married five years already. I was thirty-two, maybe thirty-three. But Hervé, he said not yet. Well, of course, he was dedicated to his job.'

I lost some of what they said but then I caught Violette mentioning *le grand projet* and working late.

'Didn't you start to wonder?'

'Not really, Fiona. It was going to be the best business park in the region. So I completely understood he had to work away from home. Anyway every Friday he came home with roses.'

'Oh – classic guilt offering!'

'Yes, I realise this now. But I was so naïve… just occupying myself, correcting the homework and being the good wife, who cooks *Moules marinière* for her husband.'

'So how did you discover…?'

'One Friday evening I met his *collègue*, in the supermarket, Auchan. Buying some yoghurts, I remember it exactly. And Bernard said, all alone, where's Hervé? And I said, he's working late on his '*grand projet*.' Well, he looked confused. So I said "Mais, Bernard – le parc d'activités! 24 hectares…" And he looked horrified and embarrassed, then he said "Mais ça n'existe pas!"'

'So it was fictitious, your husband's *grand projet*?'

'Completely. Bernard said it was just an idea they talked about with a *promoteur* for the future when the economic situation would be better. So Hervé, he told me a big lie… Tell me Fiona, do *all* men lie?'

'The vast majority… I think it's genetic.'

'Oh yes, they are so brilliant at it! Hervé…' (Bam! – slamming of a drawer) 'he is the champion du monde!'

I heard the chink of crockery, the clatter of teaspoons, then Violette's voice again, calmer, more matter-of-fact.

'Et bien, voilà, c'était une liaison.'

'An affair?'

'Yes, with the chief architect. Corinne – older than me. Can you believe it? But of course, she is the boss with the mon-ay. A very clever strategy, he got a nice promotion that way.'

She broke into French then to slate her rival. *Blonde péroxydée… le décolletage au bureau… le bé-em-doublevay dans le parking…*

'So you wanted a divorce.'

'Natur-al-ly. My husband, he betrayed me. How can I accept? So I moved to the Baie du Mont-Saint-Michel with my parents for some time… But then, even worse: I discovered Hervé had taken a lot of my savings mon-ay from our account.'

The tang of fresh coffee began wafting across the conservatory.

'The last time I saw him, you know what he had? This big, expensive gold watch and I thought: 'Gros cochon! Tu te permets un Rolex avec mon argent.' Oh yes, with *my* mon-ay!'

'Le salaud!'

'Oui, c'est un vrai salaud, c'lui-là!'

Yes, *le salaud*. Both of them seemed to enjoy unleashing that cathartic word. Of course, there was a certain irony to my eavesdropping while they were slating Hervé. No doubt Moira and 'the girls' must have gone for *me* on the odd occasion when they met in the wine bar, the only difference being the scale of misdemeanours: stress, forgetfulness, tiredness, disinterest, over-commitment to work – sure, guilty on all counts. But not infidelity, nor theft. At least I spared her those.

Simon came in to the kitchen then, chivvying up the coffee, which seemed to put a dampener on their chat. In fact, I remember wondering if the two women had gone back through to the living room. Which would have served me right for sitting there, listening like a sly fox…

'So you got a quickie divorce.'

'Well, it wasn't simple. In fact, my first solicitor, he was really unprofessional.'

'Really? Why?'

Pause in the conversation, presumably while they were pouring the coffee.

'Ironic thing, at the first meeting he seemed very polite and professional. Have confidence in me, Madame, I am here to assist you… So he persuaded me to tell him what I knew about the *adultère*: the times, the dates. Yes, he wanted to know all about *her*… and then our intimate details.'

'How intimate?'

'Well, our finances, our relationship, how often we…'

Her voice tailed off. I knew something personal was coming. Something delicate and painful not intended for my ears. But what could I do? I was trapped in my refuge.

'Then, when I was going down the stairs to the foyer afterwards, I heard his voice, my solicitor, joking to his *collègue* in the corridor – using very vulgar language: *Le mari baise la patronne* – her husband is fucking the boss! Ha ha, so funny. They laugh about it.'

'The shits! That's appalling! So then you found another solicitor?'

'Of course, I did not trust him. But you live and learn, Fiona. There are men like this. Professional, educated men with no integrity; no respect for women at all. But they smile to your face and take your mon-ay.'

'God, poor you. You've had your share... Still, at least Simon's a sweetie.'

'Yes, I'm lucky. Simon understands how to treat women...'

They took in the coffee and I sat there, finishing off the wine, trying to make sense of it all. And I began to see how the sassy Maîtresse of the contract could have emerged from a more delicate, naïve Violette, who woke up one day to find her cosy world rocked to its foundations.

It was getting on for midnight, and I was contemplating re-joining my fellow francophiles in the other room, so as not to offend the hostess. But then I heard the click of her heels on the conservatory tiles, followed by the chink of a glass. I got up from my chair.

'Having a refill Violette?'

'Michel! What are you doing?' She held her glass of rosé, looking slightly petulant. 'Hiding by the Christmas tree! Aren't you enjoying yourself?'

'Of course I am. Great food, great wine, atmospheric café songs... Quite a change from the usual new-year dos I go to.'

'Oh what are they like, then?' She was sipping her wine rapidly; a little nervously.

'Well, the food's always predictable; usually it's *done* by an outside caterer or they just get party trays – but never home-cooked *coquilles St Jacques* and *lapin au cidre* like yours.'

Of course that pleased her. Perhaps that is why she rewarded me with a clementine from the pyramid on the table.

'Pour vous, Michel: une mandarine confite. Spécialité de Nice.'

'Merci.'

It was delicious, oozing sweet nectar, but fiendishly sticky. I was aware of Madame draining her rosé, enjoying the sight of me getting messy.

'It's good?'

'Very good...but very sugary.'

She whisked across to the long table for a serviette, treating me to a glimpse of her slim waist through the diaphanous black dress.

'Voilà.'

As I wiped myself, she began adjusting one of the baubles on the tree, in the process dislodging a glittery robin. She seemed quite irritated at her clumsiness, uttering a discreet *merde* and tutting to herself as she bent down to pick it up. But then, endearingly, cajoling the bird ('petit rouge-gorge...') as she straightened the flimsy wire in its wing and returned it to its branch.

Suddenly she was conscious of me watching her:

'My God, you must think I'm crazy! Talking to a toy bird! Telling it to be'ave itself!'

'Not at all. You should hear me when my hand slips during woodcarving.'

She looked at me for a second or two, her head slightly tilted; a strange kind of look – quizzical and seemingly interested, although not overtly flirtatious.

'OK, Michel, on y va?'

In the living room *le charmant Simon* was already circulating with the champagne, the large lady in pink joking about hiring him as a butler. There was just time to grab a flute before the countdown to midnight and the toast. '*Bonne année, bonne année*' in Home Counties accents! I noticed Violette embracing Simon and his hand squeezing her waist, then I saw her knocking back her champagne. Suddenly, in the midst of rather embarrassed greetings and gauche, English style *bises*, we were interrupted by the anonymously launched rocket balloon, screaming around the room and dive-bombing our heads. I remember Guillaume gasping 'C'est un Doodlebug!' But Violette was extraordinary – open-mouthed, then shrieking as the orange sausage zoomed crazily around her for its spluttering finale.

Finally, rounding off the evening, came the singing. Just two songs, as I recall: *Alouette, gentille Alouette* with its numerous verses, followed by *Auprès de ma blonde*. For that one we joined arms and swayed side-to-side in a convivial sort of way, doing our best to sing heartily, none louder, of course, than Edouard.

I suppose it was around quarter past midnight when, in respectable British style, the *soirée* wound up. My fellow francophiles started getting their coats but I found myself letting them pass me by, strangely lethargic and feeling my head throbbing after the heavy red and the singing. On his way past me, Edouard delivered his parting words:

'Enjoyed yourself? They put on a good spread, Simon and his *concubine*.'

'Concubine?' Evidently Guillaume was as perplexed by the term as I was.

'Relax; it means common-law wife, nothing more.'

Simon was good enough to fix me a coffee while Violette was saying her goodbyes in the hallway. Dr Khan put his head round the door to wish me well, and I could hear various murmurings of appreciation as people departed – *formidable, magnifique, merveilleux*... The room was hot and airless so I took the liberty of opening the patio doors and I remember that strange mixture of exhilaration and fuzzy-headedness as I stepped outside onto frosted flagstones, feeling the cool, tingling sensation on my face.

Concubine! Is that what she was to him? Well, if the omniscient Edouard said so, who was I to argue? I suppose until that point, with the various distractions of the evening, I hadn't had time to consider the precise nature of her relationship with Simon. What was striking was how little time they spent together, one or other of them always on kitchen duty or attending to the needs of the guests. But with the seed planted in my head by Edouard, it seemed quite plausible, from the way they embraced, that she *would* be his common-law wife.

Rockets and starbursts were exploding around me in the darkness. New Year's Eve and everybody paired up – Luke and Rachel in Leeds, Moira all lovey-dovey with her new fiancé, Simon and Violette. Still, who knows, I remember thinking, maybe the coming year will be a good one, or at the very least more positive than the last.

Another rocket screamed and I was starting to feel the pinch of the cold through my shirt. It was then that the loud disco beat came thudding through the cool air – surreal waves of it, Ibiza style, louder then fading… and I turned and saw her.

She was standing with her back to the window, swaying her hips seductively to the electronic beat. I watched her take hold of the champagne bottle, the one I'd brought, fill her glass, raise it to her lips and drain the contents in a long, extravagant gesture. As I entered the room, I coughed loudly and she turned, looking startled.

'Michel! Mais je…'

'Simon's just getting me a coffee.'

'Aha.' A rather minimal reply, I thought, but then the music seemed to be preoccupying her; irresistible even, as she resumed her swaying motion to the beat.

'Tu aimes la musique disco?'

'Uh… je préfère…'

'Danse avec moi!' Her eyes insistent. 'Danse, Michel!'

What choice did I have? She grabbed my hand, pulling me towards her into the middle of the room, and then began moving her arms fluidly and wiggling her hips like a professional dancer. Of course, I did my best to pick up on her energy and keep in time with her, but all the while I was feeling awkward and leaden-footed.

'Who's this?'

I thought she muttered something improbable like Snake Town.

'Who?'

She raised my arm high and twirled in and out, with a look of exhilaration.

'J'adore!'

It was a crazy feeling; being way out of my depth, attempting to move to that fast, hypnotic club music – a disco anthem, no less. And yet, for all that, there was something sexy about the music and I was relishing the moment with Violette; relishing her dance skills, her energy and flirtatiousness, the unmistakable come-hither look as she leaned towards me and mimicked the soft female's voice: at ni-i-i-ght... Then Simon came in with my coffee and, with a curious mixture of relief and regret, I let her break free.

'Not your scene?'

The blue-eyed boy, offering me the cup with what might have been a patronising smile.

'Not really. I was into heavy rock. You?'

'Oh, *love* it. Disco, salsa, samba...' I could see him glancing over at his *concubine*, going strong by herself.

'Well, please... you go ahead – show me how it's done!'

Which, of course, he did, in Travolta style, picking up the beat and clapping energetically with Violette. Like a couple of pros they were in perfect synchrony, shimmying down and looking adoringly at each other. At one point, however, I remember she lost the beat momentarily and looked a touch unsteady on her feet, but almost immediately she recovered in time to raise her arms high and sway and chant the anthem with him, as if they were out clubbing... then shake her shoulders and everything else outrageously at him! At which point I drank my coffee, thinking: someone's in luck tonight – but not me.

As the beat faded, she came over to the table, flushed from exertion, and leaned her back against the flock-papered wall.

'Oh, c'est fatigant!'

Simon was over by the CD player. 'Let's have something quieter.'

'Oh, I know!' She broke off from trailing her fingers over the beads of moisture on the champagne bottle. '*Couleur Menthe à l'Eau*', put it on for me, darling... You know, by Eddy Mitchell.'

I found myself watching him flicking through the CDs, his long, lean back, longer and leaner even than my son's. How old was he, Madame's lover boy? Pushing thirty? Wearing a Seventies shirt that I could *just* have worn first-time round. Where on earth did he get it? Maybe it was a Christmas gift from Violette. Or maybe he *was* a catalogue model.

When I looked back, she was topping up her glass again. Even in my tired, vague state, it occurred to me that she must have downed quite a few in the past hour alone. But she seemed remarkably lucid as the opening notes of the French ballad came.

'Somebody said this song was just for me.' Wistful little smile. 'My green eyes...'

Was she talking about the lousy Hervé or maybe some other guy in the past? Why did I even care? She finished her glass and I watched her setting it on the table, slowly and deliberately, looking pleased with that simple feat of co-ordination.

'Ah, c'est bon ça!' A second later the alcohol kicked in. 'Woooh!' She began reeling and put her hands to her temples, as if to steady herself. 'Ça me fait tourner la tête!'

'Why don't you sit down?'

'No, I don't need to sit, I must look after *you*, darling.' I thought she was talking to Simon but no: she was looking at *me*, heading straight for *me*, swaying on her heels. *La charmante Violette* in her slinky dress, displaying her charms exclusively for my benefit.

'Ah Michel, le bon docteur Michel… très élégant ce soir.' She began adjusting my collar and I got the blast of alcohol. 'Tenez, vous désirez une femme pour ce soir? Tarif spécial.'

'I'm sorry?'

'Une femme? A woman tonight? Fifty pounds!' She began laughing, her eyes mischievous. 'Fifty pounds! Ha ha-ha. C'est une blague, Michel.'

'Ah, a joke…'

'Yes, of course. My god, you don't think I am like *that* do you? *Une fille de joie!*'

She stepped back and turned to lover boy.

'Hey, you know, Simon – Michel was naughty. He wrote bad words in his essay… *fille de joie, fille de numéro!*'

'Really?' Now he was looking at me suspiciously.

'I wasn't referring to Violette obviously…'

'Ah, mais j'étais choquée, Simon! Choquée! Après tout, la maîtresse de classe… du respect, n'est-ce pas?'

She fixed him with an expectant stare.

'Ah oui, absolument…'

He slid his arms round her shoulders and began steering her towards the sofa. I doubt it was the first time he'd seen her half-cut and craving attention.

'Now, what you need is a nice lie down... After all, you don't want to embarrass Michael, do you?'

'No, certainly I don't want to embarrass *any*-one.' She was leaning against the sofa, directing her confused gaze at some point on the far wall. 'Please excuse me – I drink too much, I say too much... I be'ave like I am cheap.' She gave a bitter laugh and her words came louder, more forcefully. 'But of course cheap is what you get when you treat a woman like she is nothing. A piece of shit... You ask Hervé about that. Or that disgusting man...'

'Violette!'

She began slipping back into the sofa, none too decorously, with her dress flipped back to her thigh. But she was oblivious, of course, muttering to herself, while Simon leaned over, addressing her as a little girl.

'Now, you've overdone it, haven't you? And you *know* you shouldn't have talked about things earlier... *Never* does you any good, does it?' He was adjusting her dress to restore her modesty. 'Only drags you down.'

'I say what I like!'

'That's your trouble, darling.'

He finished fussing over her and stepped aside with a look that seemed to invite me to do the good doctor bit.

'Now Violette, how are you feeling?'

'Fatiguée.'

'How many glasses have you had? Combien de verres?'

No answer.

'Have you taken anything else?'

Still no answer. She seemed out of it now, lying back and gazing at the ceiling. Her forehead was still warm from the exertion and she was breathing quite rapidly. As for the pulse,

I remember: one hundred and ten but strong and regular.

'Is she OK, Michael?'

'Well, pulse is a bit fast – but that's to be expected with the concentration of alcohol in her bloodstream. Do you think she could have taken anything?'

'No.' Vigorous shake of the head.

'OK. Let's get her onto her side. Just a precaution, in case she vomits.'

'Mais qu'est-ce que…?' She must have felt my hand on her leg.

'It's all right. We're making you comfortable.' Simon took the shoes while I bent her knees. 'Then you can have a nice sleep; you'll feel better in the morning.'

'Shall I stay with her?'

'Best thing. Put a blanket over her when she cools down and if she wants a drink, give her water, nothing stronger.'

'Absolutely.' He was looking a shade contrite. 'I'm sorry about this. It doesn't happen often, believe me.'

'Well, it's New Year after all, isn't it, Violette?'

'Hmm.' It was more of a groan than a comment.

I remember leaning over her, inhaling her heady cocktail of perfume and champagne.

'Violette, merci pour une soirée magnifique.'

'Excuse-moi…'

She was sinking back, her eyelids leaden. Then suddenly she made a supreme effort to pull herself out of it, opening her eyes wide for a few seconds. And they were tired, vague, misty but an extraordinary jade green.

'Michel…' Gazing at my face with a kind of dazed wonder!

'Yes?'

'Tu es superbe… comme un jaguar.'

CHAPTER 13

There was a brilliant moon on the eleventh of January. And it was breezy, with clouds racing dramatically across the sky. And equally dramatically, Madame was late – late enough for me to conclude that she would not be showing up at all. Well, perhaps she couldn't face seeing me after her extraordinary behaviour at the party. Unless she'd forgotten the lesson completely. By eight twenty, I was considering ringing up to find out what was going on – which would have been a perfectly reasonable thing to do, having set foot in her house, in her bedroom no less! But no – play it cool, I thought. *Que sera sera.*

So as a consolation prize I began swigging Pinot Noir and grilling the Gruyère-topped half-baguette, and I was wondering whether unreliability and poor timekeeping were characteristics of all French females, and whether our neighbours across the Channel go in for such things as New Year resolutions when dr-r-r-ring! Typical. Absolutely bloody typical! There she stood, eight twenty-seven, reporting for duty in her khaki raincoat.

'Ah, Violette! Quelle belle surprise!'

'Bonsoir, Michel.'

'Classic timing! Just when I was about to enjoy my Swiss toast!'

'Oh but you knew I was coming, didn't you?' Innocence itself as she stepped inside.

'Well, I suppose theoretically I knew it was a possibility. Much like waiting for a bus, really – you hope it might appear eventually.'

'Oh I see.' Lips parted in disbelief. 'You compare me to a *bus*!'

'Well – a glamorous bus, obviously.'

'Glamorous bus – the ridiculous idea! You know something? You are crazy, Michel! Crazeee!' A tentative smile, twitching around the corners of her mouth, and overcoming all resistance. 'Mon dieu, autobus, moi! Ha ha ha!' Throwing her head back with her nervy laugh. 'Ha-ha-ha-ha.'

Next thing, both of us were caught up in it, infecting each other with our laughter. She was captivating, doubled up then trying to regain control, eyes dancing, body trembling – outrageously petite and flirtatious and cute. How I overcame the urge to squeeze the living daylights out of her in an almighty bear hug, I'll never know.

Eventually, when we managed to compose ourselves, she was the first to speak.

'Excuse me, Michel. My mother telephoned and we had a long conversation. She worries because Papa is so tired at the moment and now he has this terrible cold. But maybe you want to cancel for tonight?'

'No, don't be absurd. Now you're here…'

At that point, some semblance of normality resumed: Madame hesitating by the coat hooks and her student offering to take her case to assist in the removal of the raincoat. After which came *la révélation*: underneath the military exterior, the riot of leopard spots!

'Wow! Is that what you call jungle chic?'

'I call it my *robe panthère*. It's a bit of fun in the winter.'

Indeed. For some reason – possibly to mark our final lesson – I suggested using the living room for a change and she agreed, choosing the armchair nearest the window. As usual, she began undoing her executive case, while, naturally, I allowed myself a further look at the dress. Stretchy leopard-print moulding itself to her figure, skimming down over her waist and hips and swishing out to just above the knee. Very youthful and flirty, and such an ingenious design, the whole thing wrapped around and tied at the side. Just one tug and she would be all undone, I remember thinking that.

When I returned with her glass of water she was sitting gracefully, extending her black suede boots, looking decidedly seductive, it must be said – and considerably more elegant than some ten days before, crashed out on the sofa in her twisted black dress. And I wondered what, if anything, she remembered of the end of the *soirée*, and whether her flirtatiousness with me meant anything or was merely the product of too much champagne?

I sat on the sofa, more or less opposite. She looked across at me.

'I like your shirt. Nice colour, *anthracite*. It looks nice on you.'

'Thanks. Actually, it was a birthday present from my son.'

'Oh, when was your birthday?'

'Back in November... the twelfth.'

'Aha. Twelve November...'

She pursed her lips, looking thoughtful, and I noticed the shiny pink lipstick.

'So, first of all, some news. Some exciting news! I am going to France this weekend for an interview for a translation job with a big Anglo-French company.'

'Good for you.'

'Yes. And I think on Tuesday they will formally offer me the contract.'

'And you'll say yes.'

'But of course! Working for a prestige organisation,

translating articles from the London office for the French company magazine – it is a good opportunity. I would be stupid to refuse.'

'Yes, it sounds pretty good.'

'Exactly. But there is only one problem with this job.' She sipped her water and smiled nicely at me. 'You see, Michel, un-for-tun-ate-ly, even if I am based in London, I could not continue with all my private students. I would have to keep just one or two.'

'Ah yes.'

Now who would they be? The impeccable Doctor Khan, no doubt, and probably fast-track Fiona.

'Anyway, we will see.' She put down the glass on the coffee table, then looked up at me with her tutor's expression. 'Now, Michel, let's evaluate your progress so far. You can talk about your home, your career, your family situation... What else? France, natur-al-ly... the places you have visited, the holidays you used to have. You understand the perfect, the imperfect tense, the *passif*... Oh yes, and you can express your opinions in writing, even on the boring subject of women's shoes.'

'Indeed.'

We exchanged meaningful glances.

'So tonight I want to talk about dreams and ambitions, using the conditional tense, I would like: *je voudrais*.'

'OK.'

'Alors, vous avez une ambition, Michel?'

'Une ambition? Ah oui. J'ai une fascination pour les îles. Je voudrais naviguer dans mon yacht, visiter les petites îles intéressantes.'

'Lesquelles? Corfu, Sicile, Corse?'

'C'est possible. Mais pour commencer, je voudrais aller... I would go?'

'J'irais.'

'J'irais à Guernsey, Herm, Alderney et aussi le petit archipel de Chausey.'

'Ah Chausey, oui, je connais.'

Of course, I guessed she would know about Chausey, being her local islands, not so far from the Baie du Mont-Saint-Michel. Despite the years since her visit as a teenager, she remembered quite a lot – the multitude of flat islets; the cluster of dwellings on the main island but otherwise the wildness, the picturesque bays, the seabirds, plunging into the water like white arrows.

'Sounds my kind of place. Like the Scilly Isles, quiet, unspoilt, away from the crowds... Chance of seeing dolphins, maybe seals. Does that appeal to you, Violette?'

'In a boat? Mm-m... perhaps.' Her finger was tracing the leopard print on her sleeve. 'Yes, it could be nice. Natur-al-ly, it depends on the weather and the boat... what kind of *yote*. For example, if it is com-fort-able with a *cabine* and *couchettes, un frigo... une douche.*'

'Naturellement.'

'And nobody will be careless and hit you with the thing, like happened to your unfortunate wife.'

'The boom? Heaven forbid!'

'Good.' A little smile, another sip of water. 'Then in that case, it sounds quite nice.'

At that moment, I confess, I had a vision of you, Violette. Fine, clear day in midsummer... You in shorts (and sensible shoes!) making your way along the pontoon at Granville marina, then coming aboard, gingerly it must be said, to learn the ropes. Then we'd be setting sail for Chausey, sea breeze on our faces, watching the small islands on the horizon growing larger by the minute. And we'd drop the hook in some secluded bay, have our picnic, relax, go for a swim...

Of course, you had no idea what was going on in my head. Although, curiously – maybe female intuition – you smiled over at me from your armchair and raised the subject of nautical sleeping arrangements.

'C'est confortable, Michel – dormir dans un *yote*?'

'Ça dépend.' Given her obvious interest, I thought I'd sketch (in English for ease) the pros and cons of fore and aft cabins and the types and configurations of berths. Even the joys of climbing over your partner to get in and out of a double one.

'But in the summer, Michel, on a warm night, you could be sleeping outside under the stars. *Dormir à la belle étoile*, we say.'

Dormir à la belle étoile... We caught each other's glances and just for a moment I felt there was a hint of promise.

After that we touched on a couple of my other ambitions – buying a place in Provence, and speaking fluent French. Even, wildly optimistically, pioneering a surgical technique one day that would carry forward my name.

Then came the moment to surprise her with my little written piece.

'Oh you did some extra work?'

'Yes, well, after all, I've had a couple of months – so I've put down some thoughts on woodcarving. *La sculpture sur bois*.'

'Oh, the carving, how interesting. Please read it to me.'

Flashback to the shoes essay, to Violette listening patiently yet ever more incredulously to what I had to say. But that was then and she was smiling encouragingly, waiting for me to begin.

'Ma passion pour la sculpture sur bois a commencé le jour de mon 50 ième anniversaire. C'était à Box Hill. Les couleurs d'automne étaient magnifiques et par serendipité, Luke et moi, nous avons trouvé une branche avec les contours fascinants.'

'So you started on your big birthday.'

'Yes, that's when I was first inspired.'

Then I regaled her with my purple prose – the best I could manage about the piece of storm-struck yew we found off the path, followed by the technical section describing the hours of graft and experimentation with the mallet and the gouges until I had completed my first piece, Torque.

'Torque? Why this name?'

'Because the sculpture was contorted, twisted.'

'Oh, I understand. Continue.'

She seemed to appreciate the artistic section of my essay with the references to Rodin (well, of course, she knew about him) and also the inimitable Henry Moore and Barbara Hepworth.

'Very good.' She looked up, waiting to hear my humble conclusion:

'Un animal, une personne, ou une pièce abstraite? Les possibilités sont infinies. C'est pour le sculpteur d'examiner une simple pièce de bois et de révéler son âme.'

Silence; long, measured silence. She was looking pensive.

'What did you think?'

'You know, Michel, it is really very good French. I didn't hear many mistakes. And for the tools and the woods you found the correct voca-bulary – bravo!'

'Thanks.'

'And the best part, Michel, was the last sentence. Not everybody can write about how they discover the soul in a piece of wood.'

'Well, how could I possibly forget? *L'âme.*'

'Good, you remember it… Now, Michel, you have described your woodcarving beautifully in your text. So – logical question:

are you going to show me your pieces?'

The deliciousness of it! Madame inviting herself, so to speak, to come up and see my etchings.

'By all means.'

She got up and moved across the room, poetry in motion in that slinky dress. As we passed the display unit, I pointed out Torque, with its sickening radial split. *La grande fissure*, she termed it.

I led the way upstairs and into the studio, which was reasonably presentable, with barely a wood shaving on the lino. Naturally, Hole-in-the-Head was the first thing to strike her. She said very little and I saw from her expression that she wasn't overwhelmed. However, she liked my 'Modigliani'.

'You have done the face so well. Long, slim... so elegant... And I like the eyes, very natural.'

'Thanks. It's one of my earlier pieces; took me months but eventually it turned out quite well.'

'Yes. So, this is your talent... But then you are a surgeon. You are good with your hands.'

'I guess there are some parallels. The need for a steady hand, a good eye, a clear head. Not forgetting, of course, your absolute reliance on precision instruments.'

She was intrigued by the various riffler files on the work bench, touching them warily with a fingertip. Said they reminded her of the dentist. After that it was only a matter of time until she homed in on the little figure at the back of the bench.

'Oh, *this one* is interesting...'

'Ah, that's an extraordinary piece of birch I found on the Common. Incredible zig-zag shape, which was crying out to be carved.'

'So you made a zig-zague girl!'

She seemed fascinated by it, commenting on the pale wood and running her finger along the curved thigh.

'So – who is she, this girl?'

Challenging look, direct into my eyes.

'Oh, no one in particular. C'est mon imagination, Madame.'

'Alors vous avez une imagination fertile!'

Ah yes, that schoolmistress tone – the one usually accompanied by the little gold spectacles. But then immediately she was surprisingly complimentary.

'I like her shape very much… Svelte, like a gymnast. So, now you just need to finish her hands and give her a face.'

She kept smoothing her finger over the blank oval.

'Actually – she's finished.'

'Finished? How can you say she is finished?' I remember her look of incomprehension. 'Poor girl, to be left so *primitif*, without a face.' She turned her back to me, leaning over the workbench, and began sliding the sylph back towards the window, presenting me with the exquisite vision of her sexy curves through the stretchy jungle cat markings. Yet when she straightened up and turned back to face me, smoothing her dress over her hips, she appeared blissfully unaware of her callipygian charms.

'But you must give her a face, Michel. Then she will be complete.'

'Ah, if only it were so simple. But facial features are the most complex. They require delicate, fine detail. One slip of the hand and she'd be ruined.'

'Oh but you are capable to do the fine detail. You did it in your Modigliani. Look!' She went over and began examining the bust. 'Look at her eyes and the way you did the hair. All the little lines. So why not do it for the little gymnast, hm?'

'Well…' I could feel myself wavering, rooting round for

excuses. 'I've moved on since I did that one, changed my style.'

'Really?'

'Yes. Become more abstract, as you can see over there with Hole-in-the-Head.'

'Hmm…'

That quizzical look she gave me as I treated her to another serving of Westover spiel: my new broad-brush approach. The contemporary look. Less is more… It was perfectly obvious that she wasn't going to buy any of it.

'Ah non, Michel, franchement, c'est bizarre, cette histoire… This talk you give me – the broad brush! You know what I think?'

'Tell me.'

'It is crap, Michel. Crap!'

I've got to say there was something delicious about hearing that word explode from her lips: crrrap!

'I see. So you don't accept what I'm saying?'

'Michel – I know when a man lies to me. I can smell it!'

Well, when she put it like that, what else could I do but tell her? Actually it was a relief, I suppose, after these months of vagueness and evasion, of being, let's say, a little economical with the truth. But even when she got the truth, there was still that expression of disbelief.

'Un accident de ski? Ca alors – c'est incroyable pour un consultant – un chirurgien!'

'Oui. Incroyable. Stupide.'

'Mais comment c'est possible? Racontez moi!'

No doubt I drifted between English and French but she didn't mind, allowing me to go with the memories. The civilised ski-ing trip to Crans-Montana with the hospital group. The exhilaration of waking up that early April morning twenty-one months ago and stepping out onto the balcony: crystal clear at eight fifteen over the Val d'Anniviers and a deep-blue sky behind the Weisshorn with its sugar-loaf glacier. And after a hearty breakfast, the walk through the forest trail with the crisp new snow underfoot. Everything felt right. It was the day to go for the black.

'La piste noire. C'était mon ambition.'

'La noire! Oh-là-là!'

Indeed. The black run at past fifty! Maybe it was an act of post-divorce defiance or maybe it was purely a mid-life thing, a sudden urge to prove something to myself. Whatever the case, I was tingling with excitement all the way up, taking in the panorama of white peaks rising up around us, the distant twist of the Matterhorn, the fabulous coronet of Mont Blanc.

'You know, Violette, the black wasn't beyond me, I'm convinced of that. But I hadn't reckoned on the pair of young Swiss smartarses on my tail – showing off and hassling me.'

'Oh the Swiss!'

'Yes, they could see I wasn't in their league… Got a kick out of carving me up, one on each side, showering me in powder snow. Very funny – except I could hardly see, and slowed down and the guy coming down behind me couldn't stop.'

'Oh my God! What happened to you?'

'My right arm took the force of it, at the wrist. Fractured the radius, it was a hell of a mess.'

'Oh, quelle horreur!'

'Still, the Swiss medics did their best; treated the open fracture, plastered me up. Then I flew home from Geneva, and for a few weeks it seemed to be on the mend but then unfortunately a tendon ruptured, in the thumb – sometimes they fray in contact with the roughened bone.'

'Oh…' Her face was a picture of squeamish distaste.

'So I had to have an orthopaedic colleague sort me out as

best he could but two operations later, the function of my thumb is still impaired. Still, on the positive side at least I can drive now.'

'But you can not carve the wood like you did before. You don't have the same finesse?'

'Exactly. Don't have the same degree of control or grip with my right hand. In fact, I have to resort to power tools for some of my carving now.'

'Yes, I understand.' Toying with the fishtail on the workbench, lining it up precisely with the neighbouring file. 'But Michel, what about your profession?'

Ah Violette, you look up at me so earnestly and ask the killer question.

'Ah yes, *that*... Basically, God only knows.'

CHAPTER 14

We went back down to the first floor in heavy silence. The sort of silence I could have used to fill her in on exactly how sickening it feels to throw away over twenty-five years worth of career in one minute. But I thought better of it. Likewise, of sharing the utter humiliation, at my level, of being incapable of surgery; of having to take a back seat while other surgeons were drafted in to perform in theatre. The ghastliness of trying to take it all in my stride – the concern of friends and family, the exasperation of the medical director, the barely concealed delight from one or two so-called colleagues.

It was almost nine. A few precious minutes left of our last lesson – enough to squeeze in one last fascinating nugget of French. But both of us seemed vacant, listless, scanning the walls and the pictures for inspiration.

'So, you cannot do the surgery.'

'I haven't touched a scalpel in over eighteen months.'

'You are not working for that time?'

'Not hands-on. Although after lengthy sick leave, I returned to consultancy work for a couple of months, tried to pick up where I left off. And I did some supervision in theatre. But it wasn't very satisfactory – there isn't room in the system for lame-duck surgeons.'

'Don't say that.'

'Well it's true. You're either in and fully functional or you're out. So for the time being they've put me on special leave, pending a decision on my future in the spring.'

'Will you operate again?'

'I'd give it fifty-fifty. No more. It all depends on the tendon that's been rerouted from my index finger into the thumb. Weird concept, isn't it? Getting the *extensor indicis* to take over the function of its old neighbour, the *extensor pollicis longus*.'

She looked over, sympathetically.

'This accident, it was terrible for you. I am sorry.'

There was a different tone in her voice – as if she might go all emotional, so no doubt I broke in with something trite and heroic along the lines of life going on and being responsible for my own fate. But then she began probing more deeply.

'Vous avez une cicatrice?'

'Une quoi?'

'Une cicatrice.'

It took a moment to click.

'Ah, cicatrix, from Latin. Is it the same spelling in French?'

'Look it up. Check for yourself.'

I had scarcely picked up the dictionary from the coffee table when she was by my side on the sofa.

'Voilà, regarde: c-i-c...' Her index finger alongside mine: 'You see?'

Cicatrice [sikatRis] NF Scar (lit. and fig.)

'Sik-at-reese...' Suddenly, incredibly, her hand taking mine; the shivery sensation of her fingertip running slowly along the fine white line. 'Beautiful word, but what does it mean? I tell you. It means pain. Being torn open. Never the same.'

She sounded raw, vulnerable and her eyes, still apparently focused on my hand, were looking beyond it or through it to some other place known only to her.

'Et vous, Violette… vous avez une cicatrice?'

'Une cicatrice, moi?' She released my hand, getting up sharply. 'If I have a scar, you think I would show you?' She was trying to make light of it, shrugging it off with a forced smile.

'Well, not all scars are visible, are they?'

'Explain.' She was frowning.

'I'm talking about the psychological kind.'

The smile was gone, her mouth set in a hard line.

'What are you saying?'

'Well, I've been thinking… Thinking about how you were at the end of the party. You sounded a little bitter – remember?'

'Oh forget it – I drank too much. It was rubbish, what I said.'

'Hardly rubbish! It was serious stuff – talking about being made to feel cheap. Look, I hope I'm not upsetting you, raising the subject.'

'Don't be ridiculous. You don't upset me.'

'Good. Then let me ask you something. When you jokingly offered yourself to me for fifty quid or whatever – what was that all about?'

'It was the champagne, I told you.'

'Really? But to pass yourself off as cheap, when you always go to such lengths to look so chic…'

'You think so?'

'Sure. I've commented, once or twice. And I've noticed how much you like that, don't you? To be admired and complimented.'

A shrug, an ironic smile. 'Why not? This is normal, to like the compliments. It is the same with every woman.'

'No, the difference with you, Violette, is that you crave it. You crave admiration more than any woman I've ever known. And shall I tell you why? Because you need to feel that men admire you and respect you – because maybe, I suspect, there have been one or two who haven't.'

She went over to *Folies Bergères* and stood there, scrutinising the bottles in the left-hand corner.

'He put his signature on the label.'

'Yes, clever touch.'

'Of course, you realise what you are doing, Michel: Now you cannot be the *urologue*, you try to be the *psychiatre*.'

'If you say so.'

'Yes, it is evident. I know you think you can analyse me, the crazy French woman!' She turned round to face me. 'But don't imagine that you are so perfect, always in control of your life and your mind.'

'I never claimed to be.'

'Aha…' She was looking pensive. 'Anyway, it's not our business to try to analyse each other.'

'No. But as it's our last time, just fill me in on a couple of things; tell me about the high heels, the wet look, the contract. The need to be la Maîtresse.'

'La Maîtresse!'

'Remember, you said it in your advert and once or twice since, and I wonder just what made you do that.'

Of course that was her cue to start gathering up her papers and the fountain pen into her case, in the same cool, efficient way as always.

'OK, so tell me about the card game. What was that all about?'

'You agreed to it. We were both responsible. Anyway, the game is history. Our time is finished now.'

'Sure.' The fool I was, expecting her to open herself up to my questions because it just happened to be our last night together. Instead she picked up her case and went out into the hallway, where she lingered, looking rather tense, evidently waiting for me to escort her down to the front door. So I found myself rambling on about my intention to keep studying, listen to the news in French – in short, the things a good student would say to the tutor at the end of a course. For good measure I threw in a casual remark about enjoying her company.

'Thank you.' Rather strained smile as she paused by the landing window. 'Ac-tu-al-ly, Michel, you are different from my first impression on the phone.'

'Better, I hope.'

'Yes... I mean to say, during our lessons in general (evidently we will forget about your bizarre essay on shoes) you have been polite with me – which is something women don't always get from professional men. *Les hommes de standing*.'

'Really?'

We started on the stairs, she ahead of me.

'Yes, I could tell you some things, Michel...'

'Go on.'

'For example, about lawyers who are disgusting hypocrites. Architects who are liars and cheats.'

She paused.

'And doctors?'

'Doctors.' She was staring at my leather jacket on its hook. 'Strange people. Molière didn't trust them and you know what, he was right; three hundred years later, what has changed? Some of them still be'ave like they are God!'

'You mean pompous specialists and surgeons.'

'Exactly. They examine you like you are an escalope. They talk to you like you are imbecile. Talk fast, never listen... and then they *fix* you for life.'

'How do you mean, for life?'

She blew a long sigh through her parted lips, as if exhaling a draught of cigarette smoke into the air.

'Well, what they do, they just take out the bit that is the problem, they sew you up, and they write a few words in code on your file, they speak maximum twenty words with you and then they send you home. *Fini*.'

'Is that the voice of experience?'

'Maybe.' She hastily avoided eye contact.

'Want to talk about it?'

She hesitated, looking awkward for a moment, then put down her case on the floor. 'All right. Yes, why not? You may not see me again... It was quite a few years ago now, not so long after my divorce. I had to go to the *gynécologue* because of too much bleeding.'

'Menorrhagia?'

'Something like this, yes. It kept happening, more and more. Then I thought it was getting better with the medicine from my doctor. But one day in the translators' office it just came suddenly, this big red flood, all over my clothes, the chair, the floor. My *collègues* were horrified. It was so humiliating.'

'That's understandable.'

'So back to the *gynéco*.'

'What was he like, I'm assuming it was a *he*.'

'Cold, clinical, knows it all: I am bleeding, thirty-five, divorced – that's sufficient, in his opinion. Well, I said, please can we try another medicine and he said, no, waste of time. You need hysterectomy. Then I dispute with him but he said it was urgent, the only solution. So what could I do? I was pressurised, no partner to support me and discuss with me. So I let him do it. My God, I was stupid.'

'No, you were desperate for the bleeding to stop.'

'Yes, it's true. But afterwards I was thinking: why didn't he try something else? With his wife, surely he would try everything. Second opinion, third opinion. But for the little woman on the list, don't bother – just take it out and do the next one.'

'And you blame him for it?'

'I blame this clinical mentality. We fix it for you. No comprehension this will change my life. Well, of course, for him it was not even one hour. For me it is eternity.'

She was looking at the floor, her face a vision of unhappiness, hands clenched at her sides. What the hell was I supposed to do? Hold her close? Leave her be? Either way I'd be doomed. So as some half-way measure, I put my arm around her raised shoulder and she accepted it, motionless, for a few seconds until she murmured '*merci*.' Then I unhooked her raincoat, assisted her with the sleeves, thanked her again for the lessons and wished her well with her interview. She nodded, seemingly composed again, and produced a resolute smile. Then, briefly and rather awkwardly, we said goodbye.

And then – what? I remember closing the door and feeling the enormous sense of emptiness, just as when the words FIN or THE END cut in too soon on the best films. As I went upstairs I was cursing myself. Why did I let her go like that, let her leave on such a downer? It wasn't meant to be like that, not after the laughter we'd experienced in that very place little more than an hour previously. We should at least have had a handshake or a kiss on the cheek, a light-hearted or optimistic comment to round things off. Instead of which, disaster.

Yes, could have, should have… Story of my life, it sometimes seems. Anyway what else to do but divert myself with the usual clear-up routine. Putting away the dictionary, filing my essay, entering *dormir à la belle étoile* into my vocabulary notebook, loading the dishwasher, rinsing out her glass and refilling mine. All the while, I suppose I was still absorbing what she had said. Hysterectomy at thirty-five, that explained quite a lot. Her reluctance to discuss her personal life with me, her misgivings over my profession, her tender indulgence with the small girl at the party. Yes, finally, and ironically on the very last evening, I'd got to see behind the façade of la Maîtresse, to the interior. Such a fragile interior with its scars, both visible and invisible.

In the living room I put on Zeppelin, seriously loud so that every vibration would go into me and numb my head. The classic tracks that instantly transported me back to carefree times. Fittingly, it was midway through *Dazed and Confused* that I heard the doorbell. Maybe it had rung several times, I don't know. But I remember, just before I opened, knowing with one hundred per cent certainty that I would find her there.

'Violette! Step in – out of the wind.'

'I forgot to give you this.'

In my daze, as she was stepping over the threshold, I must have vaguely registered the brown envelope in her hand, which must have dropped onto the floor, where I found it the next day. But what I remember of those fractions of seconds was the extraordinary, intense silence surrounding us; the two of us lost for words, as if we were in suspended animation. Yet my senses were in overdrive, absorbing every detail...

The tang of cold air on her raincoat, then the faint hint of perfume; the tawny leopard markings emerging beneath the unbuttoned military collar; the grey-green of her eyes, perfectly matching the shade of her coat; her pupils dilated, dark and wild, like those of a jungle cat; her lips parting, as if to speak, but then closing again; the wayward strand of hair falling in a loose curl over one side of her face – its surprising lightness and springiness in my fingers; the smoothness of her cheek against my hand; the pink sheen of her fading lipstick and her soft, warm, voluptuous kiss.

CHAPTER 15

La grande passion at fifty-three! Spectacular, like the blooming of the desert – and almost as unexpected when it came. Because, when I think about it, I didn't seriously expect anything physical between us – even if at the outset I did entertain vaguely erotic notions about the woman behind the advert in the Classifieds. Even if, immediately after the bizarre game, it seemed to me that anything might be possible. But, deep down, it was a mere flirtation with fantasy. A game perhaps we each secretly played in our minds, but nothing more.

Which is why when it happened, when the glorious passion suddenly erupted out of nowhere, it knocked me for six. What was I – nineteen again, on a voyage of discovery? Except this was different somehow. Because in my youth I never experienced that kind of intensity. Then it was entirely s-e-x – one-dimensional, purely physical.

Back then, could I ever have imagined the incredible excitement generated by the act of removing a raincoat? The frisson of being *allowed* to peel it off by la Maîtresse and *allowed* to let it fall, disgracefully crumpled, onto the floor. The thrill of being able, finally, to take hold of the woman who had tantalised me for months on end; tantalised me from the column of a newspaper, from the other side of my dining table, from the lamplit cosiness of her bedroom.

And the kissing – I don't ever remember it being so amazing.

Not just the kissing; the bliss, the sheer bliss of exploring her through the clingy leopard dress – the sensuous curve from the waist to the hip, the soft fullness of her thighs, the small of her back… But I remember at one point, while we were lying on the sofa, she broke off, seemingly a little distracted.

'Michel… tu me trouves belle?' Incredible tone of voice; expectancy and sensuality tinged with underlying uncertainty.

'Oui, très belle. Tu es très belle.'

'Bien.' She was obviously pleased with my answer, kissing my fingertips, then pressing them to her cheek and her neck. 'So, tell me some lovely things.'

'En français, anglais?'

'I don't care. Be romantic… be passionate… Just tell me what you feel!'

She was trailing my fingers down her throat.

'Tu es sexy, Madame Violette. Très sexy…'

'Ah oui, c'est moi!'

She got up, suddenly empowered, displaying to me in her seductive dress. 'Look. Exclusive for you, darling. Your *maîtresse de français* in her leopard dress.'

'Yes…' I remember getting to my feet and putting my arms around her from behind. 'Stunningly gift-wrapped.'

'Of course…' Playfulness in her tone as she loosened herself and turned to face me. 'Now the best part…'

She placed my hand on the loosely tied ribbon on her waist and there was no mistaking the look in her eyes. So, joy of joys, there I was, unwrapping Violette from her slinky feline skin. And underneath – how can I ever forget? She was everything I could wish for: slim and sensuous, with her smooth, pearly skin, seductive shoulders, and toned body, perfect as a sixteen-year-old's! 'Tu es belle, belle, belle…'

In that moment as I spoke, I remember there was an

incredible radiance about her, a happiness in herself and with herself and such pleasure that I obviously found her so pleasing.

'Viens, Michel.' Draping her hand towards me, drawing me close. 'Viens. Embrasse-moi.' Reclining on the sofa, like an artist's model, enticing me. 'Make me feel a million dollars… And then I will make you feel the same.'

It must have been the small hours when we went to bed, both of us still tingling with the thrill. We got under the duvet and slept, only to be awoken by the refuse lorry at around eight o'clock. Still, we made the most of the time to get to know each other, check each other out – a sort of retrospective courtship, I suppose! Both of us asking questions, trying to fill in the gaps, fired with curiosity:

'Tell me, Violette: during our sessions when you were sitting across the table from me, what were you thinking?'

'Well, natur-al-ly I was thinking how to help your French. Concentrating on your pronunciation or deciding how to lead our conversation, when to correct your mistakes, when to let you continue because you were enjoying speaking.'

'Very professional, keeping your mind firmly on grammar and phonetics.'

'Hm, well most of the time.'

'But not all of the time.'

'No. For example, once or twice, when you looked very nice in your shirt, I imagined how it would be to kiss you.'

'Ah, did you now? And did you think about it last night, during our lesson?'

She began caressing my face with her finger.

'Yes… I did ac-tu-al-ly.' Her voice, mischievous and teasing.

'Twice. The first time was when you mentioned your birthday. Twelve November – and I think: so he is a passionate one. Because Scorpios are passionate.'

'Are they indeed?'

'Oh yes.'

'Aha... And the second time?'

'It was when we talked about the word *cicatrice*. Suddenly you looked different... strange, unhappy, unsure of yourself. And I had this desire so strong to kiss your hand, kiss your scar – it nearly drives me crazy. But of course, it was not appropriate.' She broke off then, nuzzling my shoulder. 'Now, you Michel, what did you think about in our lessons?'

'Well, most of the time I was racking my brain, conjugating verbs, trying to dredge up phrases from grammar school. Trying not to sound too much like a southern Brit! But since you ask, there were one or two moments...'

'Oh, yes? Which ones?'

'Well, for example, when you arrived in that incredible wet-look dress with the zip-front, I wondered if you were wearing anything underneath.'

'Oh – did you?'

'Of course. Like any guy, I'm not impervious to such things.'

'Quelle insolence!' But I could tell from her tone that she positively loved that. For someone so wary just a few hours ago, she seemed very secure with me. Secure enough to open up about Hervé. It felt better this time, listening legitimately, as opposed to eavesdropping. At least this time I could tell her I too know how it feels to watch the shine fade from a marriage, year by year.

'Why, Michel? Why does it have to be that way?'

'I don't know. Novelty wears off, I guess. You take each other for granted.'

'I don't want that to happen with us. You know something? It is special with you. I mean it, very special. You make me feel happy… Yes, very happy. Like I must be the perfect one for you.'

'Well maybe you are.'

'No, I am not perfect.' Her voice was edgy, suddenly. 'I have nothing where there should be my *utérus*. How can I be a complete, perfect woman?'

I hadn't imagined that she would start torturing herself, so early in the day.

'Violette, I realise the hysterectomy was an awful experience. But what's done is done, as you yourself said. So don't you think it would be better to accept it? Forget the what-ifs and if -onlys and persuade yourself it was the only solution in the circumstances.'

That was insensitive and it wounded her – that was obvious from the sudden change of tone.

'But you don't know that! You cannot judge the condition of my womb, if it could have been saved.'

'No, sure. Who knows, maybe I'd have taken a different view.'

'Michel, I think sometimes there is a way to save it, yes?'

The look in her eyes, imploring me to say something and yet dreading it.

'Well, they might have tried endometrial ablation but that's not a perfect solution, either. Maybe there are other techniques, it's hard for me to say. It's not my specialism.'

'No, of course.'

'But what I really want is for you to have some peace of mind. Leave the painful stuff behind you and move on.'

'Leave it behind! Just like you did, after your accident?'

'Well, I've been trying to.'

'No, admit to me, Michel: after your accident, you fell apart.'

'I'm not sure I'd go...'

'But of course you did. Because you were this clever, successful surgeon, Mr Superman, helping all these patients to have normality in their lives, very proud of yourself – but then suddenly you could not operate any more. Total humiliation for you. You could not take it. You see?'

'I suppose so.'

'Exactly. You felt just like I did when they did this hysterectomy to me. Like suddenly you are nothing. You have no control in your life; not even of your body. So you lose your hope, your dreams and you just watch your world disintegrate around you. Didn't you feel like that?'

'Well, all right, for a while maybe I did.'

'So, you can understand how it still hurts me, when I think, in different circumstances, I could be a mother now – with a boy or a little girl. I always imagined I would be a mother one day. Always.'

'Listen,' I reached out and started stroking her hair. 'Suppose you'd had a child with your husband, it wouldn't be all roses. I can tell you, that was the most stressful part of the break-up with Moira, reaching an agreement about Luke.'

'OK, but you still have a son, a part of you that you give back to the world. You are lucky.'

'Yes. Very lucky and I would never change anything. But then, you have something many people would envy. No worries about what your kids will do when the ice-caps have melted or oil runs out... or if they'll have a pension. You're free of that; you can go to Paris just like that. Live there for a few years, do whatever you like.'

'Paris isn't everything. I've lived there before, and Bruxelles too.'

'When you were translating?'

'Yes. After Hervé, I wanted a change – go to the big city, become completely *anonyme*. Nobody knows me; nobody knows my history.'

'But also trying to find someone new?'

'Not at first. In fact, the truth is, I wasn't interested in meeting men. But eventually, by chance, I met someone. Karim.'

Oh, boy, Karim. She had a thing for him, that was obvious. Attractive, cultured law student, would-be champion of human rights. Her voice was soft when she talked about him.

'C'était un homme très intelligent. Un homme d'intégrité, de compassion et d' humanité. C'est rare, ça, l'humanité…'

A saint in other words! And it was instant chemistry – *le coup de foudre* – as they set eyes on each other, queuing up in the Louvre to see the *Mona Lisa*, no less.

'Yes, when I saw Karim, and the way he was looking at me, I knew it immediately – he is the one! Such a lovely, kind face, eyes that have the soul… And my instinct was right, he is a good person, he helps to protect the weakest ones in society; protect them from abuse, injustice… I respect him so much for that.'

The bloody nerve! Violette lying beside me in my bed, praising her heroic ex-lover.

'Yes…' – wistful sigh – 'we spent such nice weekends together. Sometimes Paris, sometimes Strasbourg.'

'So, how come you're not with him now, your Mr Wonderful.'

'You're jealous!'

'Just feeling mildly inadequate, that's all.'

'OK, I tell you the truth, Michel… We were good together, very good. He was younger than me, yes, but it was fine. In fact, he was even speaking of marriage after he would finish his law studies. But – how can I explain? Part of me, the heart, the emotion was saying yes, yes, do it! This is the best! But deep inside, my conscience was saying no. This is too much: for him to marry a woman who is infertile, to give up the possibility to ever have his own children.'

'Not everyone wants kids.'

'Oh, he did. But you know, he even said he could accept it. But his family were very traditional, from the Mahgreb originally, you know, in North Africa. It is true, they were trying to be flexible, to accept that their only son loves a woman from another culture who is older than him. But divorced – oh that was difficult for them. And even worse: how could they accept the idea of adoption or another woman carrying our child? If we married, in the end it would have broken his family, torn him apart. I could not let that happen.'

We were silent for a while and I could hear her breathing rapidly, stirred up I suppose by her memories. No wonder she was sore; forgoing her best chance of happiness and all because of an irreversible decision of a surgeon.

'So where is he now?'

'Paris. I haven't seen him for years. Last time I heard from him, he was working to represent the rights of women in *mariages forcés*.'

'Very worthy. So after Karim you decided to come to England, change of scene?'

'Yes, exactly. I thought: go to London, teach French or translate. And first of all, I rented this flat in Wimbledon, not so far from the tennis club. But then the lease finished and luckily for me, Simon was in my evening class and he offered me to stay in his house. Et voilà… l'histoire de ma vie!'

After that she went for a shower and I brought us a tray of coffee and toasted crumpets, which she found utterly delicious, especially with strawberry jam. With the sun coming through from the balcony, wrapped in my robe, she smiled and seemed suddenly filled with optimism.

'You know, darling, you are right. We must forget the past and live for the moment. Remember the positive side. After all, I have my girls, my lovely little nieces in France.'

'There you are. You've got them.'

'Yes, thank God. It's so important. I think everyone needs someone special, someone to love, to care for, and to depend on – don't you think?'

'Yes, undoubtedly.' And I remember squeezing her hand and hearing myself say: 'Well – the good thing is, you've got me now. You can rely on me.'

You can rely on me. I took it that the arrangement was reciprocal. Well, it certainly seemed a two-way thing that morning, as we got dressed, feeling at ease and so natural, as if we had been together for years. And I remember our relaxed hug and a kiss by her car – unexpected treat for the postman and any bored onlookers of Monterey Drive! Then I wished her *'bon voyage'* for the ferry trip the next day and, with a satisfied internal glow, watched her drive out of the gates. *My* Violette!

I heard from her, as expected, on Saturday – just after my leisurely breakfast with the paper. She sounded relaxed, chatting away merrily in her native tongue: rough crossing – *mer agitée* – but smooth onward drive through the Cotentin, arriving home in time for *Sole diéppoise*.

Apparently it had turned into a nice sunny Saturday and after our conversation, she was going to drive her parents up the coast to Jullouville to visit some family friends and take Papa for a short stroll along the seafront. She was looking forward to seeing the long, sandy beach of her childhood summers. More importantly, of course, there was *le meeting* in Paris, for which she had bought herself a new pair of shoes to go with a classic French suit. Yes, everything seemed to be sewn up. The translation contract was hers for the taking. A taxi was lined up to drive her to the station early Tuesday morning, so that she would arrive in plenty of time for the interview. I remember telling her to relax, stay confident but not try too hard.

'I do my best. And Michel, afterwards – the best thing, I will meet other members of the team and we are going for dinner on the Ile St Louis.'

So we had a little joke: *le petit restaurant intime*… Then she promised to go easy on the champagne and behave herself; seemed keen to reassure me of her loyalty. 'L'autre soir c'était spécial pour moi…'

'Et pour moi, aussi.'

'Bien, Chéri, je te téléphone mardi soir, si possible.'

I didn't doubt it for a minute. And to confirm my faith in her, a postcard winged its way over the Channel from the Cherbourg Peninsula to me by 09.45 Tuesday. '*Plage du Cotentin*' – view of a sandy beach with the Atlantic surf rolling in. She must have written it after we spoke on the phone.

Cher Michel
Une belle plage normande juste pour toi.
J'espère que le soleil brille à Putney! A bientôt,
Je t'embrasse, ta Violette.
PS I miss you

A handful of words, rapidly penned and yet I went over and over them. Striking use of the intimate form – *pour toi*… And she put: *Je t'embrasse* – With love and kisses, I suppose. What's more, just in case I doubted her keenness, she signed herself off as *my* Violette! So naturally that little card sat propped up on the dining table for days on end – a stunning reminder of Normandy, of course, but more especially, a reminder of you, ma chère Violette. Of *us*. But then, ironically, it seemed all the more poignant in the absence of any news from Paris.

No phone call on Tuesday evening. Not that I was unduly concerned – there wouldn't have been much opportunity to ring after the interview and the *dîner* might have been a lengthy affair. But as for Wednesday, I was surprised – no word all morning. Still, business as usual, Michael: hop on the tube, attend the lunchtime conference, then on to the gallery for the private view, keeping the mobile switched on just in case... Hah! Misplaced optimism there – not one lousy vibration in my pocket, no chance of saying '*Ah Violette! Comment ça va?*' and nipping outside for a more intimate chat. And not one solitary message for me to pick up from the landline at home.

Still, positive thinking, I thought; be a good student and listen to the CD she left in the brown envelope: '*Les secrets miraculeux de champagne*'. Yes, after multiple replays I understood virtually every word of that advanced level recording and I was looking forward to telling you that, Violette, on the phone; maybe even treating you to a little of Michel's French on the subject of the historical importance of the chardonnay grape and the *terroir and climat* of Champagne. While naturally I was also looking forward to hearing about the job offer and the new colleagues, and to getting a quick resumé of the latest delicacies served on the Ile St Louis.

Naturally, it occurred to me that there could be a technical problem with the mobile network – but surely the obvious alternative was to phone from her hotel room. Failing that, I might receive an e-mail or a fax sent courtesy of the receptionist – an enterprising solution, I thought, and one that would occur to most people. Or maybe another postcard would be coming my way soon: Eiffel Tower, Tuileries, Sacré-Coeur, any of them would have been most acceptable.

But no, sickeningly, nothing on Thursday or Friday either. *Rien de rien*. Even though I made sure I was back from my morning swim by seven thirty, just in case. I guess that is when I began to lose my cool – jumping every time the phone rang, which it did, perversely, umpteen times. And I found myself snapping at the foreign property agent who rang about some dilapidated place in the Var, and at the elderly man who had misdialled the dentist's number. Yes, and shamefully, I was less grateful than I should have been when Alison rang, out of the goodness of her heart, to remind me of the registration deadline for the spring EAU congress.

By Friday evening I'd had enough: enough of being on tenterhooks for four days, keyed up like Alexander Graham Bell waiting to hear the magical ding-a-ling. Enough of trying to divert myself in art galleries or with oenology in French or with twenty-five gruelling lengths of the pool. Enough of lunchtime conversations with my medical colleagues, enough of watching some mediocre late film on TV because it was a better option than lying awake.

So, there I was, six thirty, end of the working week, tucked away at a quiet corner table of my local pub, surrounded by Victorian prints on the wall, ferrying my dinner from the plate to my mouth, while taking stock of the various scenarios and emotions that had been occupying my mind all week. First and foremost, there was concern, obviously. Something must have happened. Perhaps Papa had taken a dramatic turn for the worse. Or, unthinkably, Violette could be the one lying in a critical condition, after some appalling accident. But no – in emergencies, somehow word gets through. Someone would have let me know, surely.

Alternatively, the Cotentin might have suffered a freak winter storm – orchards devastated, power lines down, communities cut off... But there was nothing on the news about that.

So, leaving the worst-case scenarios aside, there was room for more lateral thinking. A woman advertises herself as la Maîtresse... why does she do that? Heaven only knows but for a start, she has issues with status and power and respect. Not to mention big issues with men. She wants to have them on her terms, playing her game, by her rules – rules, of course, that only she can follow. And just when you think you might be starting to understand them, she tears up her rulebook, lets herself go, has a fling, opens herself up way too much. So then what? Shut up shop and back to the mind games. Make him wonder, make him jealous, keep him hanging on for news but give him nothing.

Yes, what a coup to be incommunicado in Paris, caught up with the new job and new faces, exciting possibilities. Lucky Violette, living it up in la capitale – shopping sprees, theatres, cabaret, looking up old friends, maybe rekindling old flames… and all the while the new admirer waits back in London suburbia like a faithful dog. The old 'treat 'em mean, keep 'em keen' philosophy coming back to haunt me…

But maybe there was even more to it than that. Enter Simon. To think, I'd kept my head in the sand, suppressing the doubt that he might turn out to be more than just a good friend. Well, it was perfectly possible – in fact, more likely than not. After all, how many women beyond student age cohabit with men on a purely platonic basis? Not many. And how many landlords and tenants go for strolls on the Common hand-in-hand, or call each other 'darling' and dance sexily in front of their guests on New Year's Eve? Not even one. Ergo: Simon must be lover-boy. In which case, what was I? Just a laugh? A one-night-stand? Well, to hell with it, maybe I should see it like that too. Think of what I got out of it: stimulation, flirtation, the thrill of the chase and the best screw I've had in many a year.

Yes, those were lousy thoughts, the thoughts of a confused, frustrated and apparently jilted fifty-three-year-old with too much time and space on his hands! The only solution, it struck me, was to blast them away on an open stretch of the A3 after the Friday evening exodus. A cheap thrill, pathetic for a man of my years – about as pathetic as buying the Porsche in the first place, as a consolation prize after the divorce. Still, the adrenaline rush worked a treat and I came home, had a couple of whiskies, then went upstairs and slept like a log.

On the Saturday, I woke early to sunshine, showered, dressed and headed out, over the heath and down Putney Hill for a riverside stroll. The Thames was steely blue and a moderate force 2 to 3 was blowing down river. A couple of guys from the rowing club were already hard at work, getting on with things, as was I, and the trickle of runners passing me by – all of us up and out and taking life by the scruff of the neck.

I should do this more often, I thought; spend more time by a big river in a big city, watch the water flowing smoothly and efficiently along its course. It's the same empowering feeling wherever you are – London, Prague, Boston. Then I remember noticing the fancy lamps on Putney Bridge and thinking they wouldn't look at all out of place by the Seine.

After exertion of course comes the reward: breakfast in the Italian café: orange juice, toasted ciabatta with mozzarella and Parma ham, and a macchiato while I perused the paper. Interesting feature on Franche-Comté – great farmhouses, stunning scenery, interesting wines and charcuterie. But too cold and remote in winter.

Then came the long homeward slog but spring was on the way – snowdrops breaking through and even the twitter of birdsong was making itself audible above the traffic. More people were in evidence now, getting on and off buses at the terminus; yes even that carbuncle looked passably better under the clear blue sky. Coming back over the heath, I noticed they had flung open the windows and doors of the pub, and I encountered Hilary in her jogging suit, looking impressed when I told her of my morning stroll, and suggesting we go for an early jog together one day.

A minute later I was turning the key, stepping over the junk mail, to the persistent ringing of the phone. Eleven-ish, exactly one week on from that reassuring call from France... It had to be Luke, of all people, at his most persuasive, wondering if there was the possibility of a cash injection to ease the pain of his credit card bill. After we'd sorted the business out, he was polite enough to stay on the line and ask about things at my end. Actually, it was a relief to talk, even if he did give me a hard time over my tale of woe. Oh yes, the ignominy of my son lecturing me on the complications of the fair sex.

'You didn't seriously think you could rely on a French woman?'

'Look, last time I spoke to her, a week ago, things were fine, absolutely fine. She even sent me a follow-up postcard from Normandy. In fact, I'd been half hoping there might have been one from Paris today. But alas, no. So now it's beyond me, Luke. And the swine of it is, I can't ring her. She didn't mention a hotel and I don't have her mobile number.'

'That's so sad.'

'Accepted. But that was the arrangement.'

(Her sculpted face, smiling at me from the interior of her car. 'Oh, you don't need it, darling. I will phone you.' And to think, I believed it!)

'Still, what I'll do, Luke, is wait until tomorrow night and if I still haven't heard, I'll ring her Wimbledon number... talk to Simon – not that I exactly relish doing that. Although come to think of it, he might not even be there. For all I know, he might be in Paris as we speak!'

'With her?'

'It's possible.'

'Right, I get it now... Basically, you're wasting time over a woman who doesn't like you enough to let you have her mobile number, who's living with another guy, right?'

'Right.'

'And at this moment she may be having an amazing time with him in France!'

'We don't know that, Luke. I said it's a possibility, that's all. Trouble is, there are so many possibilities. Maybe something's happened to her. I mean the Paris traffic is bloody awful...'

'Look, the probability of her being in an accident is minute, one in say – '

'OK, Luke, let's not go into mathematical probabilities.'

'Right, but be logical. If she's had an accident: you're here, she's there – nothing you can do about it. Still, you should have faith in French hospitals. They're supposed to be good.'

'Oh and I take it you'd be equally laid back if something happened to Rachel?'

'Maybe not. Anyway, Dad, are you going to waste the whole weekend on her like some loser? Or are you going to do something constructive, as you were always banging on to me?'

'Constructive! That's rich – I've only done a three-mile walk this morning, down to Putney Bridge and back before you even stuck your head out of the duvet! But fine, give me something constructive to do with the rest of the day... And don't suggest the rugby because I've already asked your uncle Edward but he's otherwise engaged. Although I suppose I could just grab a quick sandwich and take myself down to Twickenham...'

'Or go for a test drive.'

'Test drive?'

'Yeah. It's about time you got a new car.'

'Is that so? Well you can forget a new Porsche – in the present circumstances. Actually, when I change I think I'll go for something less flash, more roomy and practical, something I don't have to shoe-horn myself into.'

'Like another BMW?'

'Possibly... I suppose I could look into it. Get a trade-in quote. *Carrera* 4S 997, great spec, v.g.c. – I'd probably still get forty grand for it. I could get something more modest and be quids in.'

'Cool...'

And so there I was, early afternoon, patrolling the streets of Putney and Wimbledon in a succession of gleaming vehicles. Beginning with that 'Challenger tank', letting the salesman enlighten me with all the benefits: elevated driving position, traction control, flexible seating, full aircon, reversing sensor... And sure, that gargantuan thing would be ideal for towing a boat, or hauling furniture down to Provence, or stocking up with cases from the local vineyard. Not to mention coping with flash floods in the Rhône Delta. But most of the time it would be snarled up in the capital's gridlock, pumping out CO_2 and particulates – and I'd be just another king of the road in my 4-litre chariot, sticking two fingers up to climate change!

After the Chelsea tractor, the cabriolets and coupés seemed more seductive – smooth, sleek and quietly purring. And I have to say, it was remarkable how the vexations caused by the female sex seemed to melt away inside those luxurious, spacious interiors. I must have spent a couple of hours of escapism, mobile switched off, cruising the streets on that sunny January afternoon: Monsieur Dégarni in shades! Testing the soft-top and the radio – Fatboy Slim happened to be playing, so I turned it up, of course, for the keyboards. Then, of all things, the DJ segued into that disco anthem we'd danced to at the end of the *soirée*. Yes, you had to come in to it, didn't you, capricious little Madame? Just when I had succeeded in blocking you out for an hour or two, there you were, energetic, fit and flirty, in startling 3-D.

So it all came back – our incredible night together, those twelve hours of discovery… The way you could seem delicate and submissive but then, when the mood took you, dominant and mischievous. The way you would whisper in French, nice things about liking my thinning hair, saying it suited my face, made me look sexy. And your cheekiness, your little sparks of humour and fierce patriotism. But then your other side: your self-doubt and moments of fragility. Your scar that never heals.

And your beautiful eyes, intricately patterned like the cryptic wings of *Merveille du Jour*. I even forgot myself and told you that during our intimate session on the sofa, and you looked at me as if I were a nutcase!

'*Merveille du Jour*? C'est quoi, ça?'

'Un papillon, Madame.'

'A butterfly!'

'No, I mean a moth, actually.'

'Oh, so to you my eyes are like a moth! Aha, yes, all right… One moment, I just go to phone la clinique psy…'

'It's a compliment. They fascinate me, the flecks of green and grey in the iris.'

'You're crazy, Michel!'

'Am I?'

'Yes. Crazy! Dingue! Complètement fou!' Then kissing me indulgently. 'So, you know about the butterflies? Tell me, you go to catch them with a net on Wimbledon Common, yes?'

'Not now, obviously! But as a kid… So did Edward. He had bigger, brighter specimens than mine, hawk-moths and the like. I was jealous as anything. But neither of us ever caught a *Merveille du Jour*. Never even saw one.'

'Good, I am glad for it. It escaped the strange English boys like you, chasing butterflies. Before you chase the girls, ha? Not to forget the pretty nurses...'

'If you say so.'

'Hey – look at me. Regarde-moi!'

And you looked in deep and said they were nice eyes, amber-coloured no less...

On the way back from the dealers, I had a feeling in my bones that this time I would come home and find your message, sweetheart; the explanation to end all explanations. But no. Still, there were more pressing affairs to attend to. Working out trade-in deals. Comparing aesthetics, ergonomics, fuel consumption, depreciation, green credentials. Then there was the matter of consulting my personal motoring adviser in Leeds, looking at the bank balance and ordering my take-away.

On the sofa with my beef with ginger, I replayed the football report recorded from French radio weeks before:

Toujours zéro-zéro entre Nantes et Nancy... Corn-errr pour les Nantais, une longue balle... petit test pour la défense là... Alors 68 minutes passées, toujours zéro-zéro entre Nantes et Nancy ... Corn-errr pour les Canaris, bien joué... Ah, Nancy à l'attaque! Superbe! Nancy ouvre le score! Un à zéro! Un à zéro à Nancy...

It was around six-thirty when he came with the news: *le beau Simon* on my doorstep, looking rather less beau than usual; in fact, verging on scruffy in a black tee shirt and jeans. Slightly breathless, too, as he accepted my invitation to come inside.

'I came as soon as I could – been tied up at work all day... Unfortunately, I didn't have your phone number but I remember Violette mentioned Monterey Drive.'

'Ah... thanks for your trouble.'

'Well, anyway' – he looked awkward – 'I thought you'd prefer to hear the news in person.'

That was bloody awful, facing him in the hallway, trying to gauge the seriousness from his expression; trying to stop my mind racing ahead with ghastly visions of para-medics stretchering away the fatality in the Place de l'Etoile. So the strange, reassuring familiarity, somehow, of hearing the words 'hospital' and 'operation'. *Une crise gastro-intestinal* as Madame Lorance senior had phrased it on the phone to Simon that morning. That was the closest I got to a diagnosis.

'So she's in Paris, I take it?'

'No, Normandy.'

'Where – Caen, Rouen?'

'No, another place. It'll come in a minute...' He seemed nervy, plunging his hand into his pocket to find the scrap of paper to give to me. 'Here, I wrote down the hospital number. They'll be able to tell you more.'

'Cheers. Do you know when she was admitted? Did she even get to Paris?'

'Yes. I think the stomach pains started early Wednesday morning after she'd eaten out and she was taken in to one of the big hospitals for investigation. Then on Thursday she discharged herself – insisted on travelling home by train – typical Violette, hates being dictated to... Then apparently she was in absolute agony yesterday and they rushed her in, decided to open her up there and then.'

'So what's her condition?'

'Her mother said she'd come through the op all right... That's about all I know.'

'I see.'

I was on autopilot, trying to sound cool and not be side-tracked by the various possibilities – E. coli, acute pancreatitis, cholecystitis, perforated peptic ulcer…

'So you're intending to go over and visit her, I take it?'

'Oh, if I *could*, believe me, Michael, I'd be there right *now*, cheering her up. Hospitals are such godforsaken places, aren't they…? But unfortunately it's the worst possible timing: dress rehearsals all day tomorrow again, and the final run-down with the choreographer, then I'll be burning the midnight oil with late alterations and programme changes. And it's all got to be bloody perfect for Monday afternoon, when the buyers and the press descend to see the new collection.'

'So you can't make it.'

'Not a hope till Friday.' He swept back his hair and I caught the glint of bling in his ear. 'No, Great Titchfield Street is about as exotic as it'll get for me this week. But why don't *you* go?'

The toyboy, telling *me*!

'Well… it's a possibility, I suppose.'

'Yes, you go. She'd be *thrilled* to see you. I know Violette well enough…'

'Yes… Tell me, how long have been together… in the house, I mean?'

'Several years, now. She loves it, the location, the name: Sweetbriar… *très Shakespeare*, she says. And she adores Charlie, my dog – well, our dog virtually. When I pop over to Milan or Paris, it's nice to know she's there to look after him. Of course, I don't sting her for the rent.'

'Ideal arrangement.'

'Yes, suits us both. But it's flexible. I mean, she may well go to Paris. Or I might be moving…'

I guess I was surprised by his cool, laissez-faire approach to Violette in her hour of need, and the efficient domestic arrangements. Symbiotic, you could say. Whatever he was to her – landlord, housemate, dance partner, friend – he wasn't a lover. Or if he ever had been, he didn't deserve to be right now. But then it was becoming increasingly clear to me that his inclination would probably lie solely in the other direction.

Yes, it was at that point that I began to see him in a new light. No longer as a rival for the affections of Violette but just a guy who happened to have a spare room when she needed it. Someone who could take her dancing; help prepare for those magnificent *soirées*... offer tea and sympathy and discuss Paris chic like no straight guy ever could.

After he left I felt curiously elated. Suddenly, the equation could be resolved perfectly: Violette and me – and no one else. But then it struck me that this elegant solution depended entirely on the existence of Violette. I dialled the number, pumping myself up, ready to decipher the words *appendicite* or whatever came at me over the line. But the nurse was guarded with the information and fast-talking, tainted with some heavy regional accent. I got precious little of her opening words except for Madame Lorance and *un état stable*.

'Stable, c'est bon. Et pour visiter l'hôpital?'

'Bon... possible... mardi.'

'From Tuesday? Mardi?'

'Oui.'

'D'accord, j'arrive mardi. Vous dites à Madame Lorance: Michel a téléphoné, Michel Westover. Je suis docteur.'

'D'accord, c'est noté. Le docteur Westover arrive mardi.'

CHAPTER 17

Ah, ma belle Violette! What a sight you are – pale, drawn, thin, decidedly unglamorous with your nasogastric tube, limp hair and swamped by that gown. All in all, although you would shoot me for saying so, you would easily pass for mid-fifties.

Still, on the positive side, all your obs are fine and you appear to be making good progress. Saturations 97%, temperature coming down nicely. Although obviously you are still pretty wiped out – too tired to respond to my voice, except to move your head a fraction and sink back into the pillow. So while you have been out of it, I have been sitting here, despatching my *sandwich au jambon*, and tripping down Memory Lane: right back to your advert and our phone conversation; your entrance in the linen suit, the wet-look dress, the game, the party… And it all seems light years away.

Perforated duodenal ulcer! *Lésion ulcéreuse duodénal*. And to think, there I was at the party, dismissing it as a touch of IBS or dyspepsia! Now, had I asked a few more pertinent questions, and had you been less cagey about your symptoms, we might just have caught it and got things under control with medication. Still, they did a thorough job of omental patching, judging by your notes: *Réparation laparoscopique de la perforation*. Two surgeon-job apparently… Right sub-costal incision, 5 mm. *Suture synthetique. Lavage saline* 0,9%...

'Monsieur!'

'Ah, Mademoiselle!'

The nurse, crisp and efficient in her uniform.

'Ce n'est pas permis de regarder le dossier médical.'

'Ah, excusez-moi.'

Tut tut, Michael Westover. Caught in the act by a nurse! And quite right too, Mademoiselle – you update the obs chart and take the *dossier* out of harm's way. Don't stand for any nonsense from the likes of me!

So that's that. I shall have to wait patiently like a well-behaved visitor. Still, the room is pleasant enough – light, airy, scrupulously clean. Not even the hardiest *Staphylococcus* would dare show up here. Yes, you're in a decent place and you're receiving good care. I see you even have some cultured bedside reading – an interiors magazine, a couple of novels and a bookmark in elegant calligraphy, produced by some monastery I would guess. *Notre Père qui êtes aux cieux*. Our Father who is in heaven...

When did I last have cause to say the Lord's Prayer? At my own father's funeral, I guess, almost four years ago, reciting the words numbly with the rest of the congregation, barely registering their meaning. But since then... Naturally it didn't occur to me to ask for divine assistance as I lay messed up on that Swiss piste. Nor for a miraculous restoration of tendon function after surgery. And yet for some inexplicable reason on Saturday evening, just after contacting the hospital, I found myself uttering some vague approximation of a prayer. Extraordinary, involuntary thing – as I got up to go into the kitchen, the words came of their own accord and I directed them 'upstairs': let her come through.

But I might just keep that secret to myself. Wouldn't want to unnerve you! Besides, I don't know where you stand on religion. Are you Catholic, Protestant, agnostic, or even atheist? No, I'm sure you believe. Why else would you speak so passionately about the souls of the pilgrims? Yet there are so many things I don't know about you – even at the most fundamental level. Take your forenames. Violette Linné Sabine – I bet the hospital never had that combination on their records before! Linné, now that must be one of your botanist father's touches, a tribute to the great Linnaeus, I would imagine.

Oh yes, Violette, you're a bundle of surprises. Fascinating name, fascinating person, fascinating past. But there must be more to come; more of your surprises and revelations and sudden whims. How could I expect to possibly know it all, given that we've notched up less than a day in each other's company? Quite a bit less, actually. Five hours of lessons, plus some twelve hours overnight, then twenty minutes or so of *the game*, plus about the same one-to-one at the party... All of which makes a grand total of eighteen hours. Eighteen hours with capricious Violette.

Ah, here he is at last: the man himself from gastroenterology, pausing for the debrief with the nurse before he enters. Yes, he looks French: olive skin, brown hair, greying slightly. Must be early fifties, like me – we were probably doing clinicals simultaneously either side of the Channel.

'Bonjour monsieur.' Cordial smile on his part.

'Bonjour docteur. Je me présente: Michael Westover, urologue de profession.'

'Ah yes. You are the doctor friend of Madame Lorance.'

'That's correct.'

'You are working in an English hospital?'

'Yes, in central London, one of the best known...'

'Ah. So, Docteur Westover, you will understand this is a classic example of duodenal ulceration provoked by the presence of *Helicobacter pylori* and consequently we have undertaken the surgical repair.'

'Laparoscopic closure.'

'Exactly. And now our strategy is to eradicate the *Helicobacter* with the antibiotics combined with the *antisécrétoires gastriques*.'

'Well, all credit to you, things seem to be under control now. By the way, would you say it's unusual for peptic ulcers to occur in a woman of this age?'

The classically French pursed lips. 'Yes, but it can happen. As we know, *Helicobacter* is the normal cause but in addition, alcohol aggravates the condition so evidently the season of parties and *réveillons* will not help the situation.'

'Sure.'

'So, you are knowing Madame Lorance for some time?'

'We've become friends quite recently. Actually Violette's my French teacher, on and off...'

'Ah, so she is teaching you the French. Very interesting.'

Indeed. If you only knew just how interesting, Monsieur Gastro... Black wet look and FMs!

'So Doctor Westover, excuse me, I must examine Madame Lorance now, if she will wake up for me.'

'Sure, I'll step outside... Leave you to it.'

So the boot is on the other foot. Here I am, no different from the layman in the corridor, waiting for the surgeon to examine and pronounce. For at this very moment, the other side of that door, he will be undertaking the palpation and inspecting the sutures. I bet he'll have a light touch and will be drawing on his excellent bedside manner. Not a *mécanicien* by any means... In fact, quite the opposite: he's the hero of the hour who saved your life, Violette. And I suppose, deep inside, there's a little bit of envy on my part – that I wasn't able to be your hero. Still, there are those patients of mine who've been grateful for my efforts in theatre, a fair few lives extended and made more comfortable.

'Docteur Westover, nous avons fini.'

'Alors...' He looks reasonably satisfied with his patient. 'So, the abdominal examination was satisfactory. As you know, we have achieved stability on the oral fluids, and soon we will try for the solid food.'

'Great. Any idea when you might discharge her?'

'If progress will continue without complications I anticipate Madame Lorance can go home in maybe five days to one week. Then we will see her for another *endoscopie* after one month.'

'Excellent. Well, thank you for all your efforts.'

'Je vous en prie...' Quick glance at his watch. 'So, you may enter now. Your friend is waiting for you.'

Voilà: the object of my desire – awake and minus the NG tube now. Looking a little drowsy and disorientated but decidedly pleased to see me.

'Michel, c'est toi!'

Cute smile as I squeeze your hand.

'Hi. How are you feeling?'

'OK.' A rather half-hearted thumbs up. 'Sit, please.'

Your eyes are weak and grey-green today – not the incredible bright jade they were at the *soirée*. All in all, you're a completely different, faded Violette.

'So what's been going on, then? Perforated duodenal ulcer! And you had no idea?'

'No, well maybe I didn't want to...'

'Buried your head in the sand? Anyway, you're on the mend. Four days after surgery and making steady progress, so your surgeon tells me. He seems a nice enough guy...'

'Yes, he is good.'

'Hey, I've brought you a treat – some refreshing grape juice!'

The look of delight on your face. Not surprising, having been deprived of the pleasures of food and drink for days on end.

'Now, provided I manage to insert the straw in the hole… which is about as tricky as laparoscopic surgery… *Voilà!*'

'Merci.'

'Not too much – a few sips, then we'll take a break.'

No wonder your mouth is dry. It's warm in here with the low sun coming in through the blinds. Not a bad day, really, for January.

'Mm, c'est bon.'

'It's good stuff that juice – a little sugar boost.'

'Délicieux. Better than champagne!'

It's good to see you smile. There's more spirit in you already, although you're still weak, trying to push yourself up on the pillows, clearly frustrated with the IV line.

'Here, I'll help you….'

Those ribs – where did they come from? And where did your chest go? Not so much teenage as non existent! What are you now, all of forty-five kilos? A mere shadow of that sensual, beautifully upholstered body you were so proud of. To think, just two weeks ago, there you were, seemingly a picture of health and vitality: 'Exclusive… for you darling!' But don't doubt it for a second, you'll be that way again. A few weeks of convalescence.

'Michel, I feel so bad because – '

'Don't talk, if it tires you.'

'No, I want to explain. I was too busy to phone you on Tuesday. We stayed late at the restaurant. And then in the night I had this stomach pain and I was so sick. So they took me to a hospital and I stayed one and half days in Paris – all these tests. They test my breath, my blood, then they put this tube in my nose and throat. And then I go for this *endoscopie* and they discovered I have this *ulcère* which is even bleeding a little bit.'

'OK, take it easy!'

'I am OK, Michel!' One of your assertive glances there, just enough to tell me who is boss. 'Anyway they wanted to keep me in Paris but I said no.'

'You took a risk, discharging yourself.'

'Well, the pain was a little bit better for a while and they gave me the *antibiotique*, so I went back to Normandie.'

'You took a long train journey. That's crazy!'

'I was OK – well, tired but I just drink mint tea. So anyway, I arrived home on Thursday night, feeling so hot and exhausted. Immediately I go to bed… But I wanted to phone you in the morning.'

'Sure – but events intervened.'

'Yes, Friday morning – oh je continue en français, c'est fatigant de parler anglais… Alors vendredi je me suis levée vers 8 heures, j'ai pris un petit croissant et du café avec Maman, c'est tout. Et puis cela a recommencé, les vomissements, les douleurs…'

'Sharp pains?'

'Aie aie aie! Terrible. Alors, l'hôpital. Et le consultant, il a décidé d'opérer.'

'You can't mess about with peritonitis.'

'No. Very dangerous, the doctors tell me this. I could have died… like Napoleon.'

'Really?'

'Yes, they say he died because of a stomach ulcer.'

All this doom and gloom isn't exactly what you need at the moment. We should be talking positive, diverting your attention, looking to the future.

'By the way, your postcard came. Beautiful beach.'

'Yes. The seaside, take me there!'

'As soon as you're well. That fresh air, straight off the Atlantic.'

'Oui, l'air du Cotentin.'

'Ah oui… Still, while you're here I see you've got some novels to pass the time.'

'Yes, you must read some French literature, Michel.'

'Come on, Violette, I'd need to improve a hell of a lot!'

'You could do it. We will start with a small, simple book. I will help you.'

It's just like old times, you sitting there, enthusing to me about your marvellous language. Encouraging me to have a go, stretch myself.

'Oh, Michel, tu me passes ma brosse là, my hair brush please.'

Slowly, weakly, you start to brush, using your unimpeded hand, and it is incredible how the dull, flattened strands spring back to life, regain their shine.

'Better now?'

'Stunning!'

'You told me this at the *réveillon*, you remember?'

'How could I forget – the dress with the see-through panels! You looked incredible that night, dancing with Simon – I thought you were an item.'

'Oh but Simon, he doesn't go with women!'

'I realise that now.'

'Oh, Michel: pass my perfume, please – le Dior.'

Ah, I recognise this one. Sharp, tingling essence of French chic. And there you are, the connoisseur, inhaling your wrist so elegantly, as though you were on a spree in a perfumerie.

'Mmm, ça c'est bon.'

'Anything else I can help you with, Madame? How about a pee?'

'Michel!'

'Well, nothing makes me happier than knowing a patient's waterworks are in order.'

'Yes, they are in order. And when I have a need, I will ask the nice nurse, thank you!'

'Anytime. By the way, Violette, speaking in a professional capacity: when you're discharged, you'll need to make some dietary adjustments. Less alcohol, for a start. Less acidic food.'

'I know. I am not an idiot! My doctor spoke with me!'

'Fine. But I want you to promise me you'll look after yourself. Take it easy while you get your strength back.'

'I am going to stay some time with my parents.'

'That's great. I'm sure they want to look after you... Although, obviously, your father's not so robust.'

'I will not let myself be too much for them.'

Tread carefully. Don't patronise whatever you do.

'Listen, Violette: I've got a proposal. How would it be if you spend a week or so with your parents – long enough to get back on your feet, and let your mother cook nutritious soups etc – and after that we'll head down together to Provence for a couple of weeks?'

'Provence? But where?'

'Saint Rémy. Some friends of mine have a house there. Nice conversion, spacious with a sun terrace, fig trees – just the place for you to recuperate.'

'Maybe. But you know Michel, the company don't expect me to take a holiday after the hospital.'

'Sure but they'll be reasonable, given the circumstances. They wanted you for the job so they can wait till you're fit. Anyway, we'll take a laptop, so you can do some translation work down there. Makes sense.'

'Maybe. But you, Michel, what would you do?'

'Oh, I'd keep myself occupied. Go to the market, the *boulangerie-patisserie*. Finalise a list of names, contacts to try, if it comes to moving on from my present post. And I hope to do some carving – a nice piece of olive wood, if I can find one. Otherwise I'd be generally on hand to keep an eye on you, check your abdomen, see you have a good diet. I'd even cook dinner.'

'Yes?'

'Sure. So, how about it? Toi et moi et la belle Provence?'

You half-close your eyes with a wistful smile.

'La Provence, j'adore. Même en février. Les mimosas, les amandiers en fleurs.'

'It's a nice traditional house, substantial, several bedrooms. By the way, obviously I'm not assuming anything: if you want, you could have your own room. Or, otherwise…'

'Yes, otherwise?' You're looking at me with wide, enquiring eyes, just as you did during our one-to-ones, waiting for me to clarify my meaning.

'Otherwise… Alors, Madame, c'est la possibilité de la chambre avec le docteur Michel. Avec le grand lit, très confortable…'

'Le grand lit! Typical man, thinking of the bed!'

Are you teasing me? Putting on that look of indignation. Sometimes I can read you like an open book and other times you are a mystery. Yes, Violette Linné Sabine Lorance, I never know quite what you're going to serve up next.

'Give me your hand, Michel! The right one.'

'What for? Have I overstepped the mark?'

Suddenly you're being outrageous, taking my hand with that mischievous look, bringing it to your mouth, delivering your electrifying kisses.

'Hey, watch your cannula!'

'Well, I am waiting so long for you to kiss me! I am not so fragile.'

Strange thing, holding you in my arms in your voluminous gown, attempting to deliver a kiss while trying to avoid entanglement in the IV line. Of course, it has to be brief and restrained. Still, very acceptable after all this time.

'So, is that a yes to Provence?'

'Yes. It will be very lovely.'

You are looking jaded now. That little frisson of excitement has depleted your energy.

'Now – let's have you lying back on these nice, crisp pillows and you take a rest. No arguing. And you can listen while I tell you how I've been getting on with your articles on the economy and champagne. I've been making progress, you know. Even following football matches in French...'

You're making a valiant effort to look attentive but it's obvious that you are scarcely taking it in, about to doze off any moment. Still, it can wait. Right now what you need is rest. But at least we have sorted out the post-discharge arrangements – assuming, of course, you make a straightforward recovery without complications.

So, we've got a week or two to play with. If I get my act together, I could trade in the *Carrera* and fetch you in something nice, roomy but not prohibitively gas-guzzling. Failing that, we'll hire something decent. Of course, it'll be some drive down south but we could break the journey. In fact, we could go over the incredible Viaduc de Millau. And once there, you can take it easy. We'll build you up on good, healthy stuff: aubergines, artichokes, olive oil, *herbes de Provence*... monkfish, red mullet... not forgetting those marvellous *saucissons d'Arles*. While you, of course, can drink all the disgusting herbal *infusions* you desire.

We might do a couple of trips – the vineyards of Chateauneuf, Pont du Gard. And while we're down there, I might make a serious effort to find a *pied-à-terre*. A little place in the sun we can escape to whenever we like. Yes, I could see us spending quite a lot of time down there – after all, as things stand, I have no commitments. And come the summer, if my hand's strong enough, maybe we could sail together. I live in hope – you might help out with a bit of crewing. I could convert you yet…

But not so fast, Michael! Forget cruising the Med in July, stick to the here and now. For after your convalescence in St Rémy – then what would it be? Back to good old Putney! Still it wouldn't be so bad… cosy evenings in with you, Violette; being occasionally spoiled with your Normandy cooking. Who knows, you might even decide to come to live with me – become my '*concubine*'. Scandal in Monterey Drive!

Of course, we wouldn't be a perfect match – under-statement of the century! Two nationalities and cultures coming together, not to mention two fiercely independent egos! In fact, it's hard to see our lifestyles blending seamlessly, especially since you would be busy proving yourself with la compagnie, nipping backwards and forwards to Paris, while I would be kicking my heels, with the sword of Damacles hanging over my surgical career. Still, if it's over, there will be other avenues…

But some things will carry on just as now. I dare say you'll continue the dancing, Monday evenings, as often as you can make it. I'd even come along sometimes to watch you and Simon in action and I promise you, he can hold you, squeeze you, thrust his pelvis at you all he likes and I won't feel a tinge of jealousy. Who knows, I might even attempt to salsa with my two left feet.

Then, of course, there are the French lessons, which I imagine you will insist on continuing, albeit on a reduced scale – not only as a fall-back, but because it's part of you, something you get so much out of. So I imagine you won't want to let down your regulars – Fiona, Dr Khan, and the grammar school girl. You'll fit them in when you can. And as for me... Well, perhaps my personal tutor could put in a special appearance from time to time. Put on her wet-look dress or the leopard spots, with the high shiny shoes that we will not call FMs. I'd even pay her the agreed rate! And she could give me taxing articles from the French press, or test me on the past historic tense and assign me essays on French literature or equality of the sexes. She could praise me and correct me, as appropriate to la Maîtresse... Yes, life would be pretty dull without her.

Which is not to say that I understand all about that side of things, *ma chère Violette*. Far from it! For I keep wondering about that advert and that extraordinary choice of name. How did that come about? Was it the result of a carefully thought-out strategy or just a mad idea after too much champagne? Maybe Simon had a creative hand in it, wouldn't exactly surprise me. Or was it entirely your own work, the product of your wonderful, inventive mind?

Yes, there are some things I'd really like you to tell me. For example, how many hallways you ventured into as a *maîtresse de français*, with the expensive suit, the executive case and the mobile? And how many other clients signed on the dotted line of the contract?

Unless, that is, I was the only one. Yes, perhaps with your other male clients, you were completely conventional, straight down the line. Plain Violette Lorance, private language tutor. No rules to break, no penalties to pay. But with me, well I just happened to be the one to see your advert and I just happened to be the smug surgeon you thought was in need of taking down a peg or two by 'la Maîtresse'. The one who needed to learn a bit of respect. In fact, maybe I served as a kind of punchbag, representing the various 'professional' specimens of the male sex who outraged you in the past. Would I be anywhere near the truth?

Pointless exercise – sitting here, speculating on your motives, your *raison d'être*, when you are unable to shed light on the subject. Besides, to look at you now, who would believe there could be any emotional baggage, any history, when you are lying so peacefully and uncomplicated in your sleep?

So we'll save the questions for another day, when the time seems right. When you're recovering and we're relaxing in Provence sunshine, hundreds of miles away from it all. Then I'll delve a little deeper. Not that I expect you to bare your soul, of course.

But who knows? You might surprise me; you might be amused by my interest and seek to set me straight on my crazy assumption that there was ever anything meaningful behind the advertisement at all. In fact, I can picture you, looking at me, your eyes sparkling:

'Well, darling, la Maîtresse, what did it mean? I tell you: it was just a little bit of fun, that is all it was. *Un caprice, voilà.*'

And you'd shrug or give a little laugh and come over and sit on my lap and that would be it.

Or perhaps not. You might be indignant that I would have the nerve to ask such a question. Strutting over to me, hands on hips, producing your haughtiest tone:

'How dare you! You, the *urologue*, who examines the intimate parts of your patients, you think you can examine *my* life? My mind, my motivation, my decisions! Well, I tell you something, Mister Michael Westover: I can be what I want to be. *Liberté, Egalité, Fraternité* – you never heard of that?'

Oh, you could be feisty and defiant, as I know only too well… And I might rue the day I ever dared to probe the psychology of the enigmatic Violette. But somehow, looking at you now, calm and untroubled, miles away, I don't think it would be like that. For something tells me you would find another way. A very reasoned, philosophical, French way.

Yes, I have a feeling that you might just smile at me very charmingly and say:

'Some things in life, they are beautiful, mysterious… too profound for us to understand. So, therefore, we accept them exactly as they are. We respect their *sanctité*.'

And with a faraway glint in your eyes, you would speak of the secrets of the Mont-Saint-Michel… the secrets of the soul.

SOME FRENCH TERMS EXPLAINED

CHAPTER 1

Maîtresse de son sujet – Master (here Mistress) of one's subject.

Cela vous fera soixante livres – That will be sixty pounds to you.

Qu'est-ce que c'est? – (pronounced keske-say) What is it?

Ce n'est pas comme ça en France – It's not like that in France.

J'aime bien aller au pub – I like going to the pub.

Très cultivé – Very cultured.

Alors, voyons, nous sommes le 6 juillet – Let's see, we're now 6th July.

Je suis vraiment débordée – I'm really busy, up to my eyes.

CHAPTER 2

Ma femme – My wife .

Vous êtes mariée? – Are you married? Using *vous*, polite form.

Vous avez visité Paris sans doute? – You've visited Paris, surely?

Non, jamais – No, never.

CHAPTER 4

…à sept heures du soir – At seven in the evening.

Les deux parties se comporteront – Both parties will behave…

Vous aurez de belles températures – You will have high temperatures.

Racontez-moi ça – Tell me about that.

Elle se sentait isolée, un petit peu? – Didn't she feel a bit isolated?

Elle n'a pas compris – She did not understand.

CHAPTER 5

Agneau du pré salé – Saltmarsh lamb.

La rincette – Small drop of liqueur. Literally means the little rinse.

Le Cotentin – The Cherbourg Peninsula.

CHAPTER 6

Alors qu'est-ce que vous avez fait? – So what did you do?

Fraise, cassis, pêche, poire – Strawberry, blackcurrant, peach, pear.

CHAPTER 7

Ils s'appellent… elles s'appellent – They are called…

Les filles de joie. Les filles de numéro – Slang for prostitutes.

Est-il possible que les chaussures sont indicateurs…? Is it possible that shoes are indicators…?

Et franchement, je suis choquée – And frankly I'm shocked.

Phallocrate – Chauvinist.

Surtout d'un homme cultivé – Especially from a cultured man.

CHAPTER 10

Malheureusement – Unfortunately.

Ah mince – Darn; drat.

Attendez, j'ai une solution – Wait, I have a solution.

Vous voulez l'essayer? – Do you want to try it on?

En espérant avoir le plaisir de vous revoir – Hoping to see you again.

CHAPTER 11

Madame Bovary – Novel by Gustave Flaubert, published in 1857.

CHAPTER 12

Une bagnole – Slang term for a car.

Un promoteur – Property developer.

Gros cochon! – The pig!

Le salaud! – The bastard!

Tu aimes la musique disco? – Do you like disco? Uses the familiar *tu*.

CHAPTER 13

J'irais – I would go. From the verb *aller*, to go.

Le bois – Wood.

Le jour de mon 50ième anniversaire – On my 50th birthday.

Les couleurs étaient – The colours were (a past tense of *être*, to be).

Révéler son âme – To reveal its soul.

Incroyable – Incredible.

CHAPTER 15

Tu me trouves belle? – Do you think I'm beautiful?
Viens! – Come here!
Le coup de foudre – Love at first sight.

CHAPTER 16

L'autre soir, c'était spécial – The other night was special.
Je te téléphone mardi soir – I'll ring you Tuesday evening.
J'espère que le soleil brille – I hope the sun is shining.
C'est quoi ça? – What's that?

CHAPTER 17

Ce n'est pas permis de regarder le dossier – You can't look at the notes.
C'est fatigant – It's tiring.
Je me suis levée – I got up.
Même en février, les amandiers – Even in February, the almond trees.
Liberté, égalité, fraternité – Freedom, equality, fraternity. A motto dating back to the French Revolution and still significant to French people today.

ACKNOWLEDGEMENTS

The author would like to thank the following for their kind assistance and encouragement with this book. Dr D K Jones, Dr David Donaldson, Véronique Green, Michel Dauster, Gillian and Jonathan, Liz from Urology, Sue, Ellen, Nicole and 'Baba'. Special thanks to Neil and Susannah for their patience, guidance and belief in this novel over the past three years.

Coming soon...

Look out for the forthcoming companion novel by the author, S E Fitzgereld, revealing more about capricious Violette. A sequel is also in preparation. Further details are available from info@millefioripublishing.co.uk.